WEB OF SECRETS

Ernesto Patino

L & L Dreamspell
Spring, Texas

Cover and Interior Design by L & L Dreamspell

Copyright © 2009 Ernesto Patino. All rights reserved. No part of this publication may be reproduced, stored in a retrieval system or transmitted in any form or by any means, electronic, mechanical, photocopying, recording or otherwise without the prior written permission of the copyright holder, except for brief quotations used in a review.

This is a work of fiction, and is produced from the author's imagination. People, places and things mentioned in this novel are used in a fictional manner.

ISBN: 978-1-60318-124-2

Library of Congress Control Number: 2009927188

Visit us on the web at www.lldreamspell.com

Published by L & L Dreamspell
Printed in the United States of America

DEDICATION

In loving memory of my wife Diana

Web of Secrets

ONE

Miami, 1965

Ellen had a feeling Rebecca's fourth baby would be born in the middle of the night. Her last two—a girl and a boy—arrived well beyond midnight. When the phone rang just after one in the morning, she picked up the receiver and recognized Rebecca's shrill, twangy voice.

"My water broke, Miss Ellen and I'm feeling a little dizzy. Please hurry, Miss Ellen. I don't want to be alone when it comes."

"Now take it easy, girl. You've gone through this before. There's nothing to worry about. Just lie down and don't get yourself overexcited. We'll be there in a few minutes." She hung up the phone and nudged her husband lying next to her. "Doc, wake up. Wake up. Rebecca's water broke. Doc, did you hear me?"

"I heard you." He rolled over and tried to go back to sleep.

Ellen shook him again and Doc finally sat up and stumbled out of bed.

When they arrived at Rebecca's two-room shack on the edge of the Everglades west of Miami, they found Rebecca lying on the floor. She moaned as she slipped in and out of consciousness. Doc knelt and took her pulse, then looked into her eyes, which rolled back into her head.

"I'll call an ambulance," Ellen said. "She's never done this before."

"Don't!" Doc yelled. "You know we can't take her to no hospital. Let me work with her and see if I can get some response." He opened his bag, pulled out a capsule of smelling salts and waved it beneath her nose. A few seconds later, Rebecca responded, and took a couple of deep breaths. She looked up at Doc and Ellen.

"Am I going to be okay?" Her frightened blue eyes seemed a little more focused.

"Of course you are," Doc said. "You just had a dizzy spell is all. Can you feel the contractions?"

"They started right after my water broke and then I don't know what happened. I felt weak and I had this terrible pain in my head. I must have blacked out or something." Suddenly, she gave out a yelp. "I'm getting a strong one. It's gonna come soon. I can tell."

"Here, let's take her to the bedroom," Doc said. They eased her up, walked her to the bed, and made her comfortable.

Rebecca cried out and clutched her stomach as another strong contraction struck. "I can feel it coming, Doc. Can't you give me something for the pain?"

"Not just yet. Let's see how far along you are." He pulled her dress above her knees and examined her. "You're right, this baby will come any moment, Rebecca. Just try to concentrate and give out two short puffs and then a long one." He watched her as she breathed as he instructed. "That's it. Keep on doing it."

A half hour later, the baby's head showed. Doc shouted, "Push. Keep it up. Don't stop."

"You're doing fine girl," Ellen said as she wiped Rebecca's forehead with a damp cloth. "Just keep pushing."

Finally, Doc took the head and gently pulled on it until the entire baby was out. "It's a girl," he said, giving the baby a quick slap on its bottom. The infant shrieked, and Doc looked at Ellen. "We're going to fetch a good price for this one. Strong lungs, she's got." He grabbed a pair of scissors and cut the umbilical cord, then handed the crying baby to Ellen.

Rebecca let out a scream. "My head. It's hurting something awful. Do something, Doc. Everything's going dark. I'm scared. Please do something..." She lapsed into unconsciousness and stopped breathing.

Doc checked her vital signs and frantically attempted to revive her. No use. After a few seconds, he backed away from the bed and said in numb disbelief, "She's gone. I don't know what happened. Could've been a blood clot that went to the brain."

"We should've taken her to the hospital, Doc." Ellen's eyes welled up with tears. "We should've..."

"Damn it. There's no point going on about what we should've done. The girl is dead and there's nothing we can do. We gotta figure something out."

"Well, we can't just leave her here." Ellen rubbed her hands together. "When they find her, there's going to be a lot of questions."

Doc hesitated for a moment, then walked into the other room. He picked up the phone and dialed a number. "Amos, listen to me. We're over at Rebecca's. I need you to do something. Get over to our place and I'll meet you there. Hurry now. This is important. Do you understand?"

"I understand, Doc, I'm on my way," Amos said, in his peculiar Florida drawl.

His dark, coppery face barely visible in the moonlight, Amos was already there when they returned. He stood by his beat-up red pickup. He could tell by Doc's somber expression that something bad had happened. They stood outside and talked for a few minutes while Ellen took the baby inside and placed it in a crib next to the bureau on which she kept some old pictures. With tears streaming down her face, she paused to look at a small photograph of Rebecca holding her first baby.

"I'm sorry girl. It shouldn't have turned out this way. Doc did his best. You gotta believe that."

A few minutes later Doc came into the house. He poured himself a shot of whiskey, downed it, and poured himself another.

Amos had been to Rebecca's shack many times before, usually to deliver something from Doc and Ellen or to make sure she was doing okay. He knew where everything was and went straight to the cupboard in the kitchen, removed a large container of lard and set it on the counter. He cut a dishcloth into strips and shoved them in the lard to coat the pieces thoroughly. Next, he took the strips and placed them throughout the entire shack. Holding the last one in his hand, he walked up to where Rebecca lay, dropped it on top of her mattress, and lit it with the flick of his lighter. He worked quickly, moving through the entire shack and lighting all the lard-covered strips.

By the time he slipped into his truck, the fire had spread. He didn't want to look back at what he had done. Rebecca had always been good to him, but Doc was his friend and the closest thing he had to a daddy. He would do anything Doc asked. Not until a mile away did he glance into his rearview mirror. Golden flames reached into the sky. He quickly turned his eyes back onto the road and drove even faster to get away from a scene he knew he'd never forget.

Two

Thirty Years Later

Sarah drooped in disappointment. "I understand," she said, into the phone. "If you're going to be late, you're going to be late. I'll just put everything in the oven until you get home. Love you." She hung up and went back to stirring her sauce.

A few moments later, the phone rang. She put down her spoon and reached to answer it.

"Sarah? Sarah Baker?" said a man with a raspy voice.

"Yes, this is she."

"I know this may sound a little strange, considering you don't know me. But I happen to be in possession of some interesting information concerning your parents—your natural parents, that is—and I thought we might…"

"Who are you? How did you get my name?"

"I really can't tell you very much over the phone, but if you want to know who your father and mother were, meet me tomorrow morning in front of the main library. Say around nine-thirty?"

She clutched the phone. "If this is some kind of game, I'm not amused. Why can't you just tell me over the phone?"

"Look, if you want the information, you'll just have to trust me. Meet me in front of the library like I said and I'll tell you everything, and *I mean everything*." He paused, then added, "Your mother's name was Rebecca."

"How will I know who you are?" she asked, but he had already hung up.

Sarah placed the receiver back on its hook and stood there for a few moments, wondering if maybe somebody was playing a sick joke on her.

"Oh my god!" she yelled, smelling the burning sauce. She hurried to remove the pan from the stove.

Mark ate two helpings and had to resist a third of his favorite meal—fresh tomato and eggplant sauce over pasta. It didn't matter to him that the sauce had been left on the stove a little too long.

"So you think this guy was serious?" he asked, pushing his plate to one side.

"I don't know." Sarah pushed her food around her plate. "His last comment really struck me, though. It made me wonder how much he really knows."

"Well, I'll tell you one thing. I don't want you going near that library alone. This guy could be a kook…or worse. I think we better check it out before you do anything."

"But what if he's telling the truth? You know how much I've wanted to search for my natural parents. My folks didn't know anything about them. I always found an excuse for not doing anything, and I'd hate to pass up the chance that he really does know something."

Mark nodded. "I know how much this means to you, but I still think you should wait and maybe…"

"If it'll make you feel better, I'll call Dolores and have her follow me. She used to be a cop and she's never without her cell phone."

"I don't know," he said shaking his head. "I still don't like the idea of you meeting some stranger. But if it means that much, go ahead. Just make sure Dolores is close by."

Sarah smiled and twirled a hefty forkful of linguini into her spoon. "I've suddenly got an appetite."

Mark was late. He grabbed the coffee cup from the kitchen counter and took it with him. "I have to meet a new client this morning," he said, walking toward the front door. "If I get this account, you can start packing for that trip to Paris you've always talked about."

Sarah tightened the sash around her robe and followed behind him. "Go on, get out of here. And don't think I'm not going to hold you to it. I really am." She gave him a quick kiss.

"Good luck…and be careful," he said as he hurried out of the house.

Sarah returned to the kitchen, refilled her coffee, and took it with her to the bedroom.

She was half-dressed when the phone rang. Dolores sounded a little nasal. "I must have picked up a bug or something. I just took my temperature and it's about a hundred degrees. I can still make it if you really need me."

"No, you just stay home and rest. I'm sure everything will be okay. It's not like I'm meeting him in some remote place where nobody can see us."

"Well, just be careful and call me the moment you get back." She coughed and had to get off the phone.

Sarah arrived a few minutes early. She looked across the open courtyard and didn't pay attention to a young boy approaching. He had a shy smile as he timidly came up to her, handed her a note, then quickly ran off.

"Wait, who gave this to you?" she yelled. The boy ignored her and kept on running.

She read the note.

Go into the library to the section on Haitian history and pull out a book called Haitian Folklore and Superstitions. Turn to page 98. You will find what you are seeking.

Sarah looked around, then went into the building. She knew

the library well and found the book on a top shelf. She pulled it out and flipped to page 98. A small photograph of a semi-nude, dark-skinned man embracing a white woman, and a piece of paper that had been cut to fit the pages of the book fell to the floor. She picked them up and read the note.

> Sarah,
> What you are about to read is the truth. I am one of the few people who know the whole ugly story about the way you were conceived and about how your mother Rebecca was forced to give you up for adoption. Your mother was a lovely woman, but poor and uneducated.
> Your natural father was black. You were sold to a white couple willing to pay almost any price for a child. They never knew about your father, and it remained a secret all these years. It can stay a secret, assuming you do not wish me to divulge this information to anyone. All I am asking is that you give me $4,000 in exchange for my silence. How do you know I will remain silent? You don't. But I assure you, I have no intention of speaking to you ever again if only because I do not want to be exposed.
> I will contact you again to tell you how and when you should pay me. You should know that I have other photographs that are much more graphic, and I hope it won't be necessary for me to show them to anybody else. It was all part of a sick scheme by an old, greedy doctor who took advantage of your mother's ability to conceive. She got used to living on the meager allowance he gave her every time she got pregnant.
> Don't try to go to the police. I warn you that if you do not do as I say, I have every intention of revealing everything I know to people who might not be very understanding about your black father.

Sarah hesitated, then put the note and photograph into her purse and quickly made her way out of the library.

Twenty minutes later, Dolores still wore her robe when she answered the door.

"You're not going to believe what this is all about." Sarah strode into the house.

"What happened?" Dolores asked, her disheveled blonde hair hanging over her face. "Did the guy show up?"

"When I got there, a little boy handed me a note with instructions to go into the library and pull out a certain book on Haitian history. I went in and found the book, which had a note and a photograph stuck between the pages."

"What did it say?"

"See for yourself." She pulled out the items and handed them to Dolores, who read the note and looked at the photograph, then put them down on her kitchen table. "This is blackmail, Sarah. I think you should go to the police. Have you told Mark?"

"No, I was going to tell him when he got home from work. I wonder if it's true." Sarah sighed, reaching up to touch her face. She had large, slightly almond-shaped eyes and high cheekbones that she always thought made her look of Mediterranean descent.

"There's no point jumping to conclusions. For all you know this whole thing is a scam. He'd have to show you more proof than this, that's for sure. And besides, who is he going to tell? Mark? Your friends and family? I hardly think his information, if it does turn out to be true, is worth anything. Nowadays nobody cares about these things."

"You're probably right. After I talk to Mark I'll call the police and turn the matter over to them." After a brief pause she said, "It's too bad there isn't a way to find out if at least part of what he's saying is true. I've always wondered about my parents—what they were like, where they came from, and if they had other children. It would be nice to know if I have any brothers and sisters."

Dolores thought about it for a moment. "Maybe there is a way to find something out." She crossed to a desk on the other side of the room. From a stack of business cards piled high in a candy dish, she thumbed through until she found the right one. "I knew this would come in handy someday."

"What are you talking about?"

"Joe Coopersmith." Dolores handed the card to Sarah. "He's a private investigator who specializes in missing persons. I met him while I was still with the P.D. It wouldn't hurt to give him a call."

"A private investigator? Like the ones you see on TV?"

"He's one of the best. Used to be with the FBI. And he won't overcharge you like most of the PIs in town."

Sarah dropped all the information in her purse and looked at her watch. "I got so wrapped up in this, I almost forgot I had to be at the dentist right about now. Gotta run. Thanks for listening to me." She turned to leave and paused. "You really should try to stay off your feet. Maybe I'll come back later and bring you some chicken soup."

"Thanks, but I'll be all right. Just call me after you've talked to Mark. Good luck…and don't forget what I said about the private investigator."

※

Mark rubbed his temples, something he did whenever he was upset. "Don't take this the wrong way, but if there's even a remote chance he's telling the truth we wouldn't want it to get out. Would we?"

"I…really hadn't thought about it," Sarah said. "But what difference would it make if I did turn out to be part black? I mean, it wouldn't change anything between us. Or would it?"

Mark turned away for a moment, then said, "I'll be honest with you, Sarah. This thing is coming at a really bad time. You know I'm up for a big promotion, the one that's going to put us into a house on the water and maybe a boat to go with it. Can't you see that the people at the top, the ones who have the last word…well, they may decide to give it to someone else, someone who…"

"Who is married to a one hundred percent *white* woman," she said with a sting to her voice. She put her hands on her hips. "Is that what you're trying to say?"

"That's not what I planned to say. What I mean is, there are still a lot of people out there who have a problem with this sort of thing, and it just doesn't make sense to flag yourself for no reason at all." He looked at Sarah's hurt expression. "Look, I know what you're thinking. But I'm just trying to do what's best for both of us. If we give him what he wants, there's a good chance he'll go away and that'll be the end of it."

For the rest of the night Sarah said very little. Mark had made up his mind and there was no point trying to change it.

The next day, just after Mark left for work, Sarah received the call. This time the man sounded nervous, as if afraid he was being monitored. She wrote down his instructions and promised to do exactly as he requested. Then as she started to hang up, he let something slip.

"I had nothing to do with the fire," he said, almost like an apology. "I want you to know that." Then he hung up.

Three

Sarah felt out of place as she stood next to the rotting hull of a twenty-foot boat sitting near the banks of the Miami River. The mysterious caller said to meet him here and turn over the money. He also said to come alone.

For almost a half hour, she waited, keeping a watchful eye for strangers. Every time she saw a vagrant approaching, she brought her black leather purse closer to her body, and breathed a bit easier when he walked past. Occasionally, someone spoke, something crude, and then walked away as if afraid she might be an undercover decoy, not uncommon along that stretch of the river.

She was about to give up and leave when a black teenager dressed in a gray sweat suit came from behind and snatched her purse from her hand, knocking her to the ground. She quickly got up and tried to run after him, but he ran too fast; no way of knowing which of the nearby buildings he had slipped into.

When Sarah returned home, she rushed to answer the ringing phone.

"You did well, Sarah," the caller said. "You can rest assured, you'll never hear from me again." He hung up before she had a chance to say anything.

Mark arrived a few minutes later. He had been in the area close to where Sarah had been standing and observed the whole thing.

"Are you all right?" he asked. "After you tried to chase the guy, I drove around the area but couldn't find him. When I turned back around, you had already left."

"It was him." Her hands shook. "It was all a setup. He just called and said he had the money."

"You mean the guy who took your purse wasn't a mugger? What a relief. For a moment I thought my money was gone."

"Is that all you can think of?" Sarah snapped.

He put his hand on her arm. "I'm sorry. I'm just glad it's over. What else did he say?"

"He said I'd never hear from him again and then he hung up."

"Well, hopefully that's the end of it." He paused. "It would probably be a good idea not to say anything to anyone. I mean, about what the man was trying to have us believe."

"You mean about my being part black, don't you?" She glared at Mark. "What are you afraid of…that it might be true? It would really bother you, wouldn't it?"

He shook his head. "Of course not. You know I've always been open-minded about these things. What I'm trying to say is that we really don't know for sure what the truth is, not based on just a note and an old photograph. I say we forget it and pretend the whole thing never happened."

In no mood to argue, Sarah walked away without saying anything more about it.

Four

Three Months Later

A little on the stocky side, fiftyish, with a ruddy complexion and a trace of a Boston accent, the man didn't quite fit Sarah's image of a private investigator, at least not the ones she'd seen on TV.

From the very beginning, Joe Coopersmith made her feel at ease, and told her that whatever she said to him would be held in the strictest of confidence.

"Just knowing you used to be an FBI agent makes me feel better already," Sarah said, sitting across his desk.

Coopersmith quickly corrected her. "I was not an agent, I was an investigative assistant." It almost sounded like an apology. "I could have been an agent, but my bum knee prevented me from passing the physical. I spent over twenty years with the FBI and helped out on a lot of cases. But enough about me. Tell me more about why you came to see me."

Sarah filled him in on everything, from the night she got the first phone call to the day she got her purse snatched. When she finished she opened her purse, pulled out the note and photograph, and handed them to Coopersmith.

"If you're wondering why I decided to pay him, it's because of my husband. He's had a lot on his mind lately, mostly because of his high-pressure job, and he just wanted to do the best…for both of us."

Coopersmith took a moment to read the note and look at the photograph. "I'm not sure I understand what you think I can do for you. If you think this guy may come back and demand more money, you're probably better off going to the police."

Sarah shook her head. "I'd rather not do that, at least not unless it's absolutely necessary. Besides, that's not why I'm here. You see, ever since I read that note, I've thought about nothing else. I've decided I have to know the truth about my parents. I hoped you would investigate the matter and help me put this to rest, one way or another."

"Are you aware you may be opening Pandora's box? Some things are better left alone. I've seen more grief and heartache over secrets that were never meant to be revealed. Every family has them, you know."

"I'm willing to take my chances. And if it turns out my father is black…I'll be okay with it."

He leaned back in his chair and looked at her intently. "This may not be an easy case, you understand. Too many years have passed. People die or move away, records get lost. But I've tackled some tougher cases. Sometimes you get lucky and everything falls into place."

"Does that mean you'll take the case?"

"I don't want to give you a definite yes because I really want you to understand what's involved here. It may be weeks, months—before I find anything. In the end, I may just hit a dry hole and my bill will still be the same. There are no guarantees in this business."

She nodded. "I know you can't guarantee results. But my friend Dolores thinks you're the best and I've made up my mind. I want to go ahead with this. If it's not going to be with you, it will be with somebody else."

Coopersmith picked up the photograph and looked at it again. "I'll need to keep this and the note. I won't be able to do anything for a couple weeks, after I wrap up another case I'm working on."

Sarah smiled. "That's fine. I'll leave it up to you. Where will you start?"

"I'm not sure. The note mentions a doctor. I definitely want to find out more about him. I'll tell you one thing, though. Whoever wrote this is not very experienced. He took a big risk that you wouldn't go to the police. But he also asked for only a few thousand dollars to lessen that risk, all of which tells me that he isn't greedy, and he may or may not come back to ask for more money."

"I don't know why, but somehow I believed him when he said I'd never hear from him again. It was the way he said it, like he didn't want to do this. And the day before, he said something else…that he had nothing to do with the fire and he wanted me to know that. Do you think my mother died in some fire and maybe he felt guilty about it for some reason?"

Coopersmith raised his eyebrows. "It's possible. But like I said, it won't be easy and it may be a while before I find anything. Where can I reach you?"

Sarah wrote her name and phone number on a piece of paper and handed it to him. "By the way, my husband doesn't know anything about this and I'd like to keep it that way. If you need to call me, I'm usually home alone throughout the day except when I'm out running errands." She stood up and hesitated. "I don't want you to think I'm going behind my husband's back on this. It's just that he wouldn't…"

"You don't have to explain," Coopersmith said, getting up to see her to the door. He smiled. "I think I understand."

"Thanks. Call me when you're ready to begin."

Sarah didn't have much of an appetite and barely touched the pile of *arroz con pollo* on her plate. Her mind still reeled on her meeting with Coopersmith. "I just hope that Coopersmith is as good as you say he is," she said, from across the table in the middle of the restaurant.

"If there are secrets or skeletons to be uncovered, believe me, he'll find them," Dolores said. "Your biggest problem will be deciding what it is you want to do with his information."

There was a long pause. "I've given it a lot of thought and I guess I'm ready to hear the truth…whatever it turns out to be."

"What about Mark?"

"I'm not sure what's going to happen," Sarah said with a sigh. "But I'll have to let him know after Coopersmith finishes his investigation and then we'll see." She paused. "The other night, when I dozed off while the TV was still on, I opened my eyes and saw Mark looking at me—at my skin—almost like he was studying me to see if he could spot any black in me. I didn't say anything; I let him think I was really asleep."

"I think you're letting this thing get to you."

"That's not all." Sarah sighed. "He's not the same. We used to be very close, physically, and now he barely comes near me. He makes excuses and I just let it go. I guess I keep hoping this is just a phase and that things will get back to normal."

"Well, maybe it is just a phase. Have you tried talking to him about it?"

Sarah nodded. "In the beginning, after I paid the money, I tried. I could tell he was really bothered by everything that happened, but he refused to talk about it. It's as if he blames me, somehow, and we just haven't been able to put it behind us."

"So what are you going to do?"

Sarah shook her head. "I don't know. I've tried to give him enough space so he can resolve this thing in his own way. But so far, I've seen no change. If only he would just come out with it and tell me what he's thinking."

The waitress interrupted them to clear the table. "Will you be having some coffee or dessert?"

Sarah thought about it for a second, then forced a smile. "Bring us two Cuban coffees and two caramel custards."

Dolores changed the subject. "I found this neat little shop in

South Beach, just around the corner from Joe's Stone Crabs. It's got everything—antique jewelry, imported candles, fine china. You'll love it. I can't wait for you to see it."

Five

Three weeks later, Joe Coopersmith began his investigation in the reference section of the main library. The caller had mentioned a fire, so he pulled out the microfilm for the *Miami Herald* for the year 1964, the year Sarah was born, and slowly reviewed every issue. He came up with twelve fires, none of which resulted in deaths.

He then pulled out the film for 1965 and found fourteen fires, three of which did result in deaths. The victims of the first fire were two young boys who were playing with matches. In the second fire, an elderly woman had died from smoke inhalation hours after being pulled from a burning house. The details of the third fire were sketchy, and he read it with interest.

BLAZE TAKES LIFE OF YOUNG WOMAN
Firefighters responding to an early morning fire in a wooden shack near the edge of the Everglades were unable to save the life of a young woman whose charred body was found lying in her bed. The shack, which burned to the ground, was located in a sparsely populated area off the Tamiami Trail about a mile east of Krome Avenue. Authorities found no apparent cause for the blaze. A firefighter on the scene speculated that the young woman had probably fallen asleep while smoking. No positive identification has been made as yet, and it will be weeks before a medical examiner can determine the true cause of death, which in this case, may be difficult to do given the state of the badly-burned body.

Coopersmith rolled the reel forward and found a follow-up article written three weeks later. Short and to the point it quoted a police spokesperson as saying that the cause of the fire was believed to be accidental and the case was considered closed.

The city had grown too fast over the years, mostly to the west where the Tamiami Trail stretched out to the Everglades and the west coast of Florida. As Coopersmith drove further along the Trail, he saw billboards and signs that hadn't been there before and he shook his head. When he got to about a mile and a half east of Krome Avenue, he slowed down and looked for a place to stop and ask questions.

He spotted a small wooden shack set back on a patch of land surrounded by shallow swampland, and he pulled into it. As he got out of his car, a young man with a three-day growth of beard rushed out and began yelling at him. "Can't you read, Mister? The sign back there says 'No Trespassing,' and that means you."

"I'm sorry, I didn't see it."

"Are you a bill collector?" the man asked.

"Do I look like a bill collector?" Coopersmith replied, keeping a close eye on the man's left hand, which he held behind his back. "I'll just get in my car and leave." He turned to reach for the door when the young man moved closer and pulled out a gun.

"The pin's broken and it's not loaded," he said, waving the rusty-looking .38 special to one side. "But it comes in handy when collectors and other leeches come around to harass me. I lost my job six months ago and I just couldn't keep up with the bills."

Coopersmith looked at the man's bloodshot eyes and said with genuine concern, "Sorry to hear that." He paused for a moment. "You wouldn't happen to know someone who's lived around this area for the past thirty years, would you?"

"Who are you looking for?" the young man asked, his guard still not completely down.

"Well, to tell you the truth, I'm not really sure. I'm a private investigator and I'm looking into something that happened in

'65. A fire destroyed a shack somewhere around here and I'd like to know more about it."

"What's so important about an old fire?"

"I'm trying to put some pieces of a puzzle together for a client whose mother may have died in that fire."

The man put his hand in his pocket and looked down for a second. "My dad. He's lived along the Trail for almost forty years, maybe longer. But he's not feeling well and he doesn't like talking to strangers."

Coopersmith reached into his pocket and pulled out a twenty-dollar bill and held it out in front of him. "I just want to ask him a few questions. I promise I'll be brief."

The man snatched the bill and said, "Come on in. He's sitting in his wheelchair."

Coopersmith followed the young man into the shack and saw his father sitting in the wheelchair, watching television. "He's a little hard of hearing and his mind is not what it used to be," the young man said. He moved his father's wheelchair around so he could face Coopersmith.

"The man wants to ask you a few questions Pa," the young man shouted into his ear.

"What? What?" The old man's pale, unshaven face contorted into a frown.

The young man reached down to shut off the TV. "I said the man wants to ask you a few questions." He turned to Coopersmith. "Go ahead. Ask away. Just speak up so he can hear you."

"A shack burned down somewhere around here and a woman was killed." Coopersmith spoke loud and slow. "It happened back in 1965. Do you remember anything about it?"

The old man didn't respond and Coopersmith repeated his question. The old man shook his head a few times and finally said he couldn't remember.

"Sorry he couldn't help you," the young man said as he saw Coopersmith to the door.

"It was a long shot. Too many years have passed. Thanks for

letting me talk to him." Coopersmith left the shack, got into his car, and continued down the Trail. He had heard of a barbecue place just east of Krome. He needed a beer.

He saw mostly tourists who had come in to sample what the sign said was the best barbecue on the Trail.

Later, when he got up to pay his check, he asked the cashier the same questions he asked the old man in the wheelchair. Not surprisingly, she didn't know anything. She was a transplant from up-state New York, in Florida less than a year.

A bald, stoop-shouldered man sitting near the register got up and followed Coopersmith. He watched him get into his car and drive away. The man took down his tag number, then walked over to a pay phone and made a call. "I'm over at the barbecue place on the Trail, and I thought you'd like to know that someone's been asking questions about the old shack that burned down."

"Who is he?" asked a raspy voice on the other end.

"I don't know, but I got his tag."

"Check it out and let me know what you find."

The man hung up the phone and went back inside to finish his barbecue.

Coopersmith returned to his office and made a few calls, mostly to old friends from the Bureau, former investigative assistants like himself. In a tough case like this, he needed all the help he could get. He'd learned a long time ago that it was better to split his fee with a fellow PI than sit in his office scratching his head for new leads. He didn't have much luck except for a tip about a retired nurse who'd lived near the Trail for years and who'd worked with almost every doctor in that part of town. Harriet Peterson lived in a nursing home in North Miami—the same nursing home where his wife died of Lou Gehrig's disease five years ago. The memories of his wife, in pain and unable to care for herself, were still fresh in his mind, and he wished Harriet Peterson had been anywhere but there.

When he walked into the home the next day, he saw a few familiar faces. It made him feel better. After a brief visit with the head nurse, who remembered him well and asked how he was doing, he strode down the hall to Harriet's room. She lay in bed with her head propped up against two pillows. She sat up fully alert when he walked into the room.

"I didn't mean to disturb you," Coopersmith said as he approached. "My name is Joe Coopersmith, and I wondered if I could ask you a few questions."

Harriet narrowed her eyes. "What kind of questions?"

"I'm a private investigator and I'm looking into something that happened about thirty years ago. I was told you knew all the doctors who lived or worked along the Tamiami Trail. Do you recall any of their names?"

"Of course," she said, her voice revealing a quickness that belied her eighty-plus years. "My body may be old and worn out, but my mind is still sharp as a tack. I worked with a lot of doctors in my time, and I can tell you a few stories about them. Back then you didn't have as many specialists as you do today, which in my opinion was a better system. Most of them were general practitioners and people went to them for everything from a bump in the head to an ingrown toenail."

"What were some of their names?"

"I was getting to that. Let's see…Doctor Johnson, Doctor Ramirez, Doctor Perry and Doctor Brenner. I worked with all of them. I even assisted Doctor Lou Morgan one time when he had an emergency near the Miccosukee reservation. I went with him that day because he was desperate for a nurse and I said I'd help him."

"Was he also a general practitioner?"

"He used to be, before he lost his license. Then he started helping women deliver their babies at home. Come to think of it, I don't know what happened to him. He was older than me, so he may have already passed away. Had a nice wife, as I recall."

Coopersmith chatted with the old woman for a few minutes longer, then left and headed back to the Trail. She had given him a good lead, and he was anxious to talk to the old man in the wheelchair again.

Six

Sitting on a well-worn sofa in the living room of his trailer, Stanley Morrison shook his head and mumbled something under his breath. Then he said to Sam, sitting across from him, "I don't like it. I don't like it one bit."

Sam gulped down the last of his beer. "Well, I wouldn't worry about it, he can do all the poking around that he wants. He isn't going to find anything."

"I'm not so sure," Stanley said, picking up a glass of watered-down Scotch. "If Coopersmith is as good as you say, we've got to be prepared."

"What did you have in mind?"

"I don't know. I'll have to think about it. Right now, just keep an eye on him and let me know what he's up to."

Sam got up to leave. "I almost forgot to mention that Coopersmith used to be with the FBI. Not that it's a big thing, but I thought you'd want to know."

Stanley didn't say anything. He took a sip of his drink. He hadn't figured on Sarah hiring a private investigator. What did she want? Was she afraid he'd ask for more money? Whatever, it was something else to worry about. And the last thing he needed: something else to worry about.

"You sure it was him…Doctor Morgan, and not some other doctor?" Coopersmith asked the old man sitting in his wheelchair.

The man blinked a few times and nodded. "He took good care of my daughter and helped her so she wouldn't have the baby. She was only sixteen and we didn't know what else to do."

"Did he help other girls who had the same problem?"

"The Henderson girl who lived close to town. Her…and maybe one other girl. I can't remember her name."

"Do you recall a girl named Rebecca? She may have died in a shack that burned down."

The man shook his head. "It's been too many years."

Coopersmith didn't want to press his luck. The man had told him what little he knew. He thanked him and his son, Jimmy. On the way out, he pressed a twenty-dollar bill into Jimmy's palm.

Later, when Coopersmith returned to his office, he found Sarah waiting for him in the hallway. By the look on her face he knew she had something on her mind—something serious.

Almost immediately, Sarah apologized. "I'm sorry I have to do this, but I've thought it over and I want you to stop the investigation. I'll pay you for your time plus a generous bonus. I'm sure you probably turned down other cases to work on mine."

"I'm not sure I understand. I thought you wanted to get to the bottom of this. If it's a question of money…"

"It's not the money. It has to do with my husband and me. The other day we actually sat and talked about this whole thing. For so long he didn't want to discuss it, which quite frankly had caused some tension between us. But now, well…I'm not so sure that finding my roots is all that important anymore, especially if it means risking a marriage that up until recently had been a pretty good one. I don't always agree with my husband, but I love him very much and…"

"No need to explain. It's your prerogative."

"Well, that's all I had to say." She got up to leave. "I wanted to tell you in person because you've been very understanding and I didn't want you to think I called it quits for any other reason."

Coopersmith got up and walked her to the door. "I'll prepare a report and mail it to you in a couple of days."

"That won't be necessary. Your bill for your services will be enough." She hesitated. "Did you…find anything?"

Coopersmith nodded. "A few things. Mostly old information that needed to be checked further." He opened the door. "If you change your mind, just give me a call and I'll pick up where I left off."

Sarah smiled and he closed the door behind her. Secretly, he hoped she would change her mind, but wouldn't count on it.

Later, as he prepared to leave, the phone rang. He picked it up on the first ring. It was Jimmy from the shack on the Trail. "I don't know what's going on," he said, "but a man stopped by a few minutes ago. Don't know his name, but I've seen him around a few times. He asked if anyone had been by asking questions. I didn't much like his manners, so I didn't tell him anything."

"What did he look like?"

"Average, between fifty and fifty-five, completely bald."

"Look, I'm not sure what's going on myself. But just to be on the safe side, don't tell anyone about what your father and I talked about. Call me if the guy shows up again."

Coopersmith put the phone down and leaned back in his chair. Someone was on to him. Maybe he was getting close to something, something that meant he was on the right track. He stood to leave. The case was over. No point wasting time on it, not when he had other cases he'd put aside to work on Sarah's case.

SEVEN

Stanley Morrison worried about his health and tried not to drink too much, though it was hard not to considering the stress lately—a sick wife, medical bills, and more recently, a private investigator asking too many questions. As he had done every day for the past five months, he got up early and saw to his wife's needs: emptying her bed pan, bathing her with a sponge, forcing her to eat a little oatmeal or pieces of fruit. He used to consider himself a lucky man, when he was young and his wife was the prettiest girl he'd ever met. But that was a long time ago, before the bottom fell out from under him. His disbarment from the Florida Bar—the last straw. He really never recovered from it. He thanked God for Sam, who stood by him throughout the years. He didn't know what he would've done without him.

"You didn't shave today," his wife said as Stanley removed the bowl of cereal and sat beside her. "Is anything the matter?"

"No, nothing," he said unconvincingly. "I didn't sleep well and I just forgot to shave." He reached over and began to stroke her white, wispy hair with his hand.

"I'm never going to get better. I wish you'd reconsider what we talked about."

"You put those thoughts out of your mind. What that doctor in Michigan is doing is wrong. It's the pain that's making you talk this way. Tomorrow when I see the doctor, I'm going to ask him to give you something stronger." He paused, then changed the subject. "Did I tell you I ran into Henry and Irene yesterday? They asked about you. They want to come visit."

Emma managed a weak smile. "I miss them, especially Irene. You'll have to tell them I'm not up to seeing anyone, though."

Stanley expected her to say that and just kept stroking her hair, gently and rhythmically. Now and then he whispered soft, soothing words to help distract her mind from the constant pain. When he heard the phone ring, he got up to answer it in the living room.

Sam calling with an update. "He probably talked to old man Hollingsworth, but I'm not sure how much he found out. I still don't think he'll learn anything. Just the same, I'd rather be safe than sorry, if you get my drift."

There was a long silence. "You know I didn't mean to hurt anybody," Stanley finally said. "I hope this doesn't get out of control. I don't know what I'd do if…"

"Leave it to me, Stanley. You just take care of Emma and I'll do whatever is necessary."

Sam's last words lingered in Stanley's mind as he hung up. He stood there for several moments. When he heard his wife call out to him, he straightened up and hurried back into the bedroom. "I'm coming," he yelled. "I'm coming."

"I'm so glad we decided to meet here," Sarah said, her wide eyes taking in all the interesting items displayed throughout the store. "You were right. This place is unusual."

"That's what I like about it," Dolores said. "It's eclectic, like me." She led the way toward the back of the store where the antique dolls were kept. "I used to collect dolls when I was a little girl. I still have a couple hidden away someplace."

An old coffee mill caught Sarah's eye. "Mark would like this. Maybe I'll surprise him with it."

"You still think you did the right thing?" Dolores asked.

Sarah hesitated. "I really think Mark and I have put this

behind us. He's like his old self and I'm happy with my decision. I mean…why should I jeopardize something that means so much?"

"But you're closing the door to your past, Sarah. Who your parents were and where you came from shouldn't make any difference if the two of you are really meant to be together." She looked down. "I'm sorry. I'm butting in again, like I said I wouldn't do."

Sarah put down the coffee mill and changed the subject. "Oh, look at these." She pointed to a vase of silk flowers across the isle. "They look almost real, don't they? I've never seen anything like them."

When they left the shop a few minutes later, Sarah turned to Dolores and said something she hadn't expected to say. "The truth is, I'm not sure if Mark really meant all the things he said. But I have to give him the benefit of the doubt because I really do love him. Just because I'm curious about my past, I don't want to be the one who caused it to go sour."

Dolores started to say something, but she held back and instead offered to treat Sarah to a cup of coffee. "There's a little cafeteria down the street. They're not Cuban, but they make the best Cuban coffee this side of Little Havana."

Eight

Coopersmith hated bridges, especially ones over water. When he saw the end of the seven-mile span in sight, he breathed a little easier and pressed down on the accelerator to get there faster.

He had spent the better part of a day in Key West looking for a missing girl from Chicago. A look-alike, it turned out to be. It happened a lot in his line of work, especially with young girls who fit the general description: white, thin build, brown hair, brown eyes and a pretty smile.

By the time he reached Key Largo, he had crossed the last of the long bridges. He'd be home by sundown. Just a few more miles and *no more bridges* he thought as he followed the curve away from the island and down the last stretch of road between the upper keys and the Florida mainland. He was traveling at just above the limit when he spotted a dark blue Camaro in his rear-view mirror. He also saw a white van in the distance coming toward him. The Camaro barreled along at a fast clip, so he slowed down and moved slightly right to let it pass. When the Camaro came up beside him, it suddenly veered right and smashed into his side. His car slid sideways, over the shoulder and off the road. He lurched the wheel left to pull the car back onto the road. No sooner had he done so when again the Camaro smashed into him. This time the Camaro swerved and lost momentum. At the same instant, the driver of the white van braked, skidding sideways into the path of the Camaro. The impact was quick and severe.

Coopersmith got out of his own car and rushed to the wreck. The man lay still conscious. He tried to speak, but he was in shock and he didn't make sense. "She's sick, very sick," he whispered. He bled profusely from a deep gash in his bald head. "He did it for her. Tell him…tell him I was only trying to help."

"Tell who?" Coopersmith asked, leaning closer to him.

"Morrissss…" the man said, before he gasped and stopped breathing.

Paramedics arrived quickly, followed by the cops who questioned Coopersmith for almost an hour. Shaken, he waited a few more minutes before he got back on the road. As he drove further and further away from the scene, he wondered if the man who was killed was the same man who'd spoken to Jimmy back at the Trail. Did someone try to send him a message? It sure looked that way.

In the morning he drove over to Jimmy's shack on the Trail. He knocked, but got no answer. He could hear the TV playing and tried the door. It was unlocked, he let himself in.

"I tried knocking," Coopersmith said as he approached the old man from behind.

The man turned around and recognized Coopersmith. "You gotta help my son. The cops took him last night. They said he beat up some woman, but they're wrong. Jimmy wouldn't hurt anyone."

Coopersmith turned down the TV.

"Please help him, Mister Coopersmith. I'm all alone and I don't know what to do. Can you find out what's going on?"

"I'll check it out," Coopersmith said, nodding. "If there's a way I can help, I'll be glad to do it."

"Thank you," the old man said.

"In the meantime, try not to worry. It may not be as bad as you think." He looked at the man for a couple of seconds. "Listen, the reason I'm here is because a man I saw yesterday mentioned the name Morris, and I thought maybe you might know who he is. Maybe he lives around here."

"Do you know a first name?"

Coopersmith shook his head. "No, that's all I got. This Morris may have a wife or someone close to him who's very sick, if that's any help."

The old man thought about it for a moment. "Morris. Morris. Could it be Morrison?"

"Could be." Coopersmith shrugged.

"There's a fellow I used to know. His name was Morrison, Stanley Morrison. Did taxes, accounting, that kind of thing. As a matter of fact, I saw him with his wife at the Tamiami clinic about six months ago. She looked bad, really bad. Hadn't seen either of them in years."

"Do you know where they live?"

"Years ago, they lived in a trailer off the Trail just before you get to the city."

Coopersmith asked the old man a few more questions, but he didn't know much more, except that Morrison used to be an attorney. "You've been a big help. I'm not sure if Morrison is the guy I'm looking for, but I'm going to find out." He folded a twenty-dollar bill, and dropped it in an empty ashtray, and turned to leave.

"Don't forget about my son," the old man yelled out.

"I won't." Coopersmith turned and walked out of the shack.

Coopersmith headed east toward Morrison's trailer; his beeper went off. He pulled over to a pay phone to call the number. It was the missing girl's mother. "I just spoke to her!" the mother said. "She sounded afraid and confused. I asked her location and she said she was at a pay phone near the Sunshine Motel, off Flagler Street. Please go to her. There's no time to lose."

"I'm on my way." He slammed the phone down, jumped back in his car, and sped toward the city. He knew the motel, but it was miles away.

By the time he got there, he saw no one near the pay phone

except an old Cuban woman waiting for a bus. In his best Spanish, Coopersmith asked if she had seen a young girl hanging around near the phone.

"*Si, si,*" the old woman said. She described how a man with long blond hair and bad teeth picked her up in a red Honda. "I don't think she wanted to go with him, but he pulled on her arm and he made her get in."

"Which way did they go?"

"That way." She pointed toward downtown Miami.

Coopersmith got back in his car but didn't get very far. He hit a red light less than a block away and another one a few miles further. By the time he passed 27th Avenue he knew it was hopeless. They could have gone in any direction—north, south or all the way into the downtown area. He was approaching 12th Avenue and slowed down behind a car attempting to make a left turn. From the corner of his eye he spotted a red Honda leaving a gas station on the left side of the road. Could this be the one? He sounded his horn to make the car in front of him move faster, but the driver took his time and waited for the traffic to pass before making the turn.

Impatient, Coopersmith swung around him, wheels screeching, and tried to catch up to the red Honda moving fast up 12th Avenue. He was at least four car lengths behind, but he had it in sight. The driver of the Honda came up to a bridge as the gate lowered. He gunned it just in time to make it across to the other side. Frustrated, Coopersmith pulled over to the side and parked there. He had her, and then he lost her. That was all he could think of.

Coopersmith spent the rest of the day working on a missing person's case that involved a wealthy lady from Palm Beach. A big-bucks case, which meant the Morrison lead would have to wait. He had already figured that the lady really wasn't missing. She liked to run off now and then to have a good time in Miami, which in her case, meant getting laid by the first good-looking Latino who offered to buy her a drink. In between going from one bar to another, he made some phone calls and learned that the witness against Jimmy was his old girlfriend, a waitress named Millie who worked the day shift at a diner on Biscayne Boulevard. On his way to check out a tip at a hotel off the 79th Street Causeway, he stopped at the diner and spoke to her.

"If you're not a cop, why are you so interested?" She poured him some coffee from across the counter. She had thick brown hair tied back in a pony tail and wore heavy makeup to cover small pockmarks on both cheeks.

"I'm a friend and I'm just trying to help him."

"Look, what I told the cops is the truth. Jimmy's a hothead and he was drunk. When I told him to leave he wouldn't, and that's when he started beating on me."

Coopersmith saw the bruises under her eye and around her neck. He also noticed an old, two-inch scar just below her ear. "He did that too?" he asked, pointing to it.

"I…cut myself trying to trim my own hair. That was a long a time ago."

He didn't believe her, but didn't say anything. "I think I've found out what I wanted to know." Coopersmith stood, getting ready to leave.

"What's going to happen to him?" she asked, with a hint of concern.

"He'll probably do some time for this. The courts are getting pretty serious these days. Domestic violence, battered women. That's all you hear about in the news." He paused for a moment. "But if he really did this to you, then, friend or no friend, he deserves to stay in jail." He paused again and pulled out a couple of bucks and left them on the counter. He could tell by the look on her face and the way she bit her lip that she held back something. He didn't want to press her…at least not just yet. "Call me if you want to talk." He dropped his card on top of the two bills.

The tip turned out to be a good one. The woman sat in a corner room facing the bay in a small hotel off the 79th Street Causeway. She had checked in the night before, accompanied by a good-looking man at least ten years younger. When Coopersmith knocked on the door and nobody answered, he offered a maid pushing a cleaning cart five bucks to check out the room.

"I'm a friend of hers and I just want to make sure she's okay."

The maid hesitated for a moment, then took the money. She pulled out her key and opened the room. The woman lay on the bed nude and passed out, with an empty bottle of gin by her side. Her Latino lover had vanished along with her purse and her jewelry.

"My goodness," the maid said, trying to hide her embarrassment. "Your lady friend seems to have had a little too much to drink." She placed a blanket over her and shook her a couple of times. "Are you all right, ma'am?"

The woman, who looked to be in her early forties, gave out a moan and tried to open her eyes.

"Better get in here, Mister. Your friend's waking up."

"I'll take it from here." Coopersmith gave the maid another five dollars and waited for her to leave.

The woman sat up and stared at Coopersmith standing at the foot of the bed. "Who are you?" she asked, only mildly curious. She brushed her long, flowing hair away from her face which looked taut as though she'd recently had a facelift.

"I'm Joe Coopersmith. Your family hired me to find you… and take you back home." He picked up her dress from the floor and dropped it on the bed. "Why don't you put it on and we'll be on our way. I'll be right outside when you're ready."

"What if I don't want to go home?"

"Look, my job was to find you and take you back. If you don't want to go, I'll call them and…"

"What's the hurry?" She flung off the covers then waited for a reaction from him. She got up slowly and sauntered across the room to the bathroom. "Just give me a minute. I want to freshen up."

"Sure," Coopersmith said, barely able to hide his discomfort.

He couldn't help but notice that for a woman her age, she had the body of a twenty-year-old.

The woman was a chatterbox, and Coopersmith mostly listened to her and occasionally nodded as they drove north on the turnpike. In a way he felt sorry for her. She was typical of the women from Palm Beach, the ones who had too much time, too much money, and were over the hill—which meant over forty. He'd never been comfortable around rich people, especially women and he wondered how a guy could ever fall for one of them. *The rich are different from us*, he remembered reading someplace, and nothing was truer than in Palm Beach, a place only seventy miles due north but light years away from everything common, wild, or gritty like you saw every day in Miami.

"You know, you wouldn't be halfway bad-looking if you got a new suit and lost a few pounds." She smiled as they pulled into the driveway of her oceanfront mansion.

Coopersmith chuckled. "Take care of yourself, Miss Pennington."

"Call me Trudy. By the way, you're the first PI who's brought me back without having tried anything." She paused and then added, slyly, "Not that I would have minded."

Her father had been expecting them and stood by the doorway wearing an irritated look on his face. He walked up to the car, helped her out, and waved Coopersmith off, like he would dismiss a pesky waiter.

"Just for that, I'm tacking an extra hundred on the bill," Coopersmith muttered under his breath. He waited until they were inside the house and then pulled out of the driveway and headed back to Miami.

Nine

There was something about a fresh, chewy bagel that made getting started in the day a little bit easier. Coopersmith wasn't superstitious, but he swore that whenever he missed his bagel, the day just didn't seem to go right.

When the phone rang, just after nine, he took a quick sip of his coffee and reached over to answer it. It was Millie, from the diner.

"I had a feeling you'd call." Coopersmith wadded a piece of bagel in his mouth.

"I thought about what you said, about Jimmy having to stay in jail, and I want you to know that I didn't tell the cops the whole truth."

"What did you leave out?"

"The fact is, Jimmy came to see me that night and he *was* drunk, but he left after I told him to leave. It was a good thing, because Max, my boyfriend, came home a few minutes later. He noticed the ashes from Jimmy's cigarette on the ashtray and he just went crazy and started accusing me of cheating on him. If Jimmy had still been there, he probably would have beat the hell out of him. Instead, he beat me. Later, when he went to the bathroom, I called the cops. I wish I hadn't because he got furious with me. Don't you see, I had no choice. When the cops showed up I had to tell them something, and…"

"And so you blamed it on Jimmy."

"I'm sorry I did it. Now I don't know what to do. Can you help me, Mister Coopersmith?"

"You're going to have to tell the cops the same thing you just told me. You know that, don't you? And they may charge you with filing a false report."

"Look, I don't have much money, but I'll pay you for your services."

"Save your money. You may need it for a good lawyer. In case you forgot, I'm supposed to be Jimmy's friend, who, by the way, is still sitting in jail."

"I'm sorry, Mister Coopersmith, I didn't know who else to turn to. You seemed like a fair man. I mean, you didn't come down hard on me, like someone else would've done."

Coopersmith was a softy, especially when it came to women like Millie—desperate, sometimes foolish women who seemed to have a penchant for always being with the wrong man at the wrong time. "Look, I know a few people at the Miami-Dade P.D. I'll talk to them and see what I can do."

"I really appreciate this, Mister Coopersmith. I know I shouldn't have done what I did, but…"

"Give me a couple of days and I'll get back to you. If everything works out, you owe me a cup of coffee."

After he had hung up, Coopersmith shook his head. He'd done it again—gotten involved in something that wouldn't generate a fee.

On his way to the trailer court where Stanley Morrison supposedly lived, he stopped by the Miami-Dade P.D. and talked with an old friend, a woman named Jessica who worked with victims of domestic violence. Together they went to see the detective in charge of Jimmy's case.

A real victim's advocate, Jessica argued that no matter who had beaten her, Millie was still a victim of abuse. Her actions, therefore, were explainable because of Max's hold over her. The detective grew sympathetic and promised to convey Jessica's assessment of the case to the state attorney. Meanwhile, he wanted to see about releasing Jimmy from jail.

After leaving the P.D., Coopersmith made a quick phone call to Jimmy's father to give him the good news. He made another one to Millie at the diner and told her about his meetings with Jessica and the case detective.

"I'm not sure what's going to happen, but I have a feeling they're going to give you a break." He paused for a second. "By the way, that cup of coffee you owe me…can you throw in a bagel?"

Millie laughed and said she'd have it waiting for him.

Later, when Coopersmith pulled into the trailer court, he wasn't sure what to expect. As far as he knew, Stanley Morrison was just a name. He didn't want to make too much of it until he had a chance to ask him a few questions.

Up ahead, he saw a mailman walking toward him. He stopped and rolled down his window. "I'm looking for Stanley Morrison's trailer."

"At the end of the street," the mailman said. He pointed in the direction of the trailer. "Trailer Six B, with the wooden pelican out front."

"Thanks," Coopersmith said, rolling up his window. He drove to the trailer, parked off to one side, and got out of the car.

As he walked up to the door, he noticed someone peeking through the blinds. He pretended he hadn't seen anything and stepped up to ring the bell.

Seconds later, an old man with a thin, haggard-looking face slowly opened the door. "What do you want?"

"My name is Joe Coopersmith and I wondered if I could talk to you for a moment. You *are* Stanley Morrison, aren't you?"

Morrison seemed to recognize Coopersmith's name and immediately assumed the worst. "I don't have to talk to you. You're not the police and I know my rights."

Coopersmith felt lucky. He had found the dying man's friend.

He didn't want to blow it by saying the wrong thing. "You're right, you don't have to talk to me, but your friend—the one who died in that accident—told me something and I thought you'd want to know what he said."

"You…talked to him before he died?"

Coopersmith nodded. He had to let on that his friend had told him more than he did.

"You might as well come in." Morrison's face looked drawn and resigned. They took a seat at the kitchen table where the morning dishes sat untouched, and the newspaper sat opened to the page showing the pictures of the fatal crash north of Key Largo.

"Your friend tried to kill me, Mister Morrison. We both know why, don't we?" Coopersmith said, trying to bluff some answers from him.

"As God is my witness, I never meant to harm you and neither did Sam. He probably just wanted to scare you."

"Well, he did a good job. But it was all for nothing. I was off the case. Too bad he didn't know that."

"Sarah hired you, didn't she?"

"She wanted to know about her past." Coopersmith paused when he saw Morrison's lips quiver, as though he were about to break down and cry. "Why don't you tell me about it?"

"I don't know where to start," Morrison said, after a long sigh. "When my wife got sick and there was no money for the doctor and the treatments, I had to do something. Since the day I first met her, she's been the love of my life. I don't know if you're married, Mister Coopersmith, but when you love someone like I do, well, you'll do anything for them. Don't you see? I was desperate, and it occurred to me that people would pay to keep a dark secret from ruining their lives."

"And so you blackmailed Sarah."

He nodded, looking down at the table. "I'm so ashamed. To think I would sink so low as to extort money from a poor, innocent woman. But I needed the money and I rationalized there was no other way. After I got the money, I just couldn't..." He shook his head.

"Couldn't what?"

After a long silence Morrison leaned forward. "What I am about to tell you is something I'm not very proud of. In a way I'm glad it's over because for too many years I kept it all bottled up inside. In the beginning—and I'm talking about years ago, when I was just starting my law practice—I naively thought I helped people. Couples who couldn't have any children. I was supposed to make sure they had a lot of money and that they could keep their mouths shut when they got the baby they could never have on their own. Of course there could be no trace of it, for their own protection as well as my own."

"I assume Doctor Morgan delivered them."

"If you know that much, you know he did more than that. He controlled everything. It was his idea from the very beginning. When he and his wife picked up Rebecca to give her a ride to Miami, they felt sorry for her, at least Doc's wife did. She was a poor, uneducated girl from Alabama, who could barely read and write. She was homeless and hadn't had a good meal or a decent place to sleep in a long time. Well, to get to the point, Doc and his wife took her in and gave her a job as a maid to help around the house. She became accustomed to Doc's generosity and I guess she didn't want it to stop." He shook his head. "She had everything she needed except...the love of a young man close to her age. That's where Amos came in."

"Amos?"

"He was a young black who worked for Doc doing odd jobs. Doc practically raised him, and the young man grew very loyal to him. Anyway, he hung around the house a lot and I guess one thing led to another. When Rebecca told Doc she was pregnant, he got furious...at both of them. At first, he wanted to kick her out of the house. But his wife persuaded him not to. That's when he moved her to an old shack he owned off the Trail."

"The one that burned down?"

"Yes. Everyone assumed she died in the fire, but she was already dead when the fire started."

"But the newspaper accounts said…"

"I'm telling you what really happened." He looked out the window for a moment. "Right after Rebecca gave birth to her baby, which looked more white than black, Doc called me and told me his plan. He wanted to sell the baby to a couple who couldn't have children. He asked for my help, and I reluctantly went along with it. It wasn't hard finding a childless couple, desperate to pay any amount for a new-born infant."

"What about Rebecca? Didn't she want to keep her baby?"

"Of course. It was her baby. But she was very timid and she basically went along with it, convinced by both Doc and his wife that it was the best thing to do, for her and the baby. The poor girl barely had a chance to hold him before they took him away. He went to a good Christian couple from Lakeland."

Coopersmith still had a lot of questions, but waited patiently as Morrison took a moment to rub his eyes, which looked irritated and red, like he hadn't gotten much sleep the night before.

"I'm not trying to excuse what I did, Mister Coopersmith. Although I have to admit, I felt like I gave joy to that childless couple. They had paid a lot of money for it. Maybe that was the problem."

"What do you mean?"

"When Doc got his share of the money, it changed him, somehow. A few weeks later he told me about his idea for Rebecca to have another baby. I was stunned at the suggestion. I tried to talk him out of his crazy idea but he didn't want to listen. All he could think about was the money he would make off some desperate childless couple."

"How did he plan to convince Rebecca and Amos to go along with his little plan?"

"Rebecca was an emotionally weak girl. One way or another he would've convinced her. Don't forget, by that time she had gotten used to the things he gave her and she didn't want to give up what little she had. As for Amos, he would have done anything Doc told him to."

Coopersmith leaned back in his chair and shook his head. "How many babies did Rebecca give birth to?"

"She had four, all by Amos. All were placed without any problems…except Daniel."

"What happened to him?"

"It's an ugly story," Morrison said with a sigh. "You see, when Daniel was born he was too dark skinned. No way a white couple would accept him, especially back then. Doc was furious, as you can imagine, and he basically left me to handle the problem."

"So what did you do?"

"I had a few black clients and it wasn't hard for me to place him. Of course, I didn't get any money for him. Excuse me for a moment." He got up and went to get something from another room.

He returned holding a large folder which he placed in the middle of the table. "Everything you want to know is in that folder. Even though Doc warned me not to keep any records, I always did. Being a lawyer, it was more of a habit than anything else. It's all there…names and addresses of all the couples who adopted the infants and even some current information about the children as adults." He stared at the folder. "I used to call them my little white lies, because that's how I saw them."

"Did you blackmail anyone else, besides Sarah?"

"After I got the money from her, I couldn't bring myself to do it to the others. As much as I needed the money, I just couldn't. Sam knew everything and basically did all the legwork. He was a good, loyal friend to me and my wife." He looked away for a moment, then fixed his eyes on the folder. "There's something else," he said haltingly. "I don't know how to say this…"

"Just take your time."

"By now you probably don't think very much of me, and I really can't blame you. Once when I went to see Rebecca, I took advantage of her. But there's more as you'll see in the folder. Doc had this idea to take secret photographs of Rebecca and Amos while they were in bed together. He made copies of these photographs and sold them for a few dollars at the local bars. I wanted nothing to do with this and told him so."

Morrison looked like he wanted to stop, but Coopersmith couldn't resist asking more questions.

"You'll find all the answers in that folder," Morrison said somberly. "I knew one day the truth would come out and I wanted to have a record of it. Legally, an unwise decision, but that's another matter. You probably should know I kept a duplicate folder in an office I used to have before my wife got really sick. Someone broke in one day and stole it."

"Did you report it to the police?"

"Yes, but nobody did anything about it." His wife's moans could be heard coming from the bedroom, and he abruptly stood up. "I suppose you'll have to report everything I've told you to the police."

Coopersmith nodded. "It may not be as bad you think."

Morrison knew better, and stood there as Coopersmith reached for the folder and walked out of the trailer. After a few moments, he went to the bedroom, picked up a gun from his nightstand, and sat down on the bed next to his wife.

"Everything's going to be okay." His voice faded to almost a whisper. "Everything's going to be okay."

Coopersmith was approaching the exit gate when he heard the first gunshot. Seconds later he heard the second one, and he pulled over and looked back in the direction of Morrison's trailer. He sat there for a few anguished moments, then slowly drove out of the trailer court.

Six Weeks Later

Coopersmith had been to the morgue before, usually as support while a client identified a friend or a relative. It had never bothered him. Until now. Maybe it was because she was so young or maybe it was the way her throat had been slashed with such force that huge chunks of flesh were missing. "I've seen enough," he said as he stepped away from the body. He had compared her features with a photograph her mother had sent. No doubt about the identity.

On his way home, he thought about the girl's mother and how to break the news to her. He knew she'd have questions. Lots of questions, for which he'd have no good answers. Maybe he'd wait to call her in the morning. Yeah, that's what he'd do. People take bad news better in the morning, he always heard. He really didn't believe it but it was late and he felt in no mood to explain to her how he had her in sight and then lost her because of a rising bridge, a lousy fucking bridge. Sometimes he hated this business.

Ten

"You're on the air," said Hal Brewster, the smug-sounding host of the popular radio show in Atlanta.

"I'm a long-time listener and a first-time caller," said the voice on the phone. "I just want you to know your show is like a breath of fresh air. It's good to hear somebody telling things the way they really are. Those liberals in Washington and all their friends have fooled half the country, and nobody's doing anything about it."

"Well, you know, it didn't happen overnight," Brewster said. "Oh, no. It happened slowly, and you want to know why? Because good people like you and many others who work hard and pay taxes have trusted our elected officials—and I'm not just talking about those in Washington—to do the right thing. Don't you see, those *bureaucrats* who are supposed to look out for the welfare of everybody, not just certain so-called *disadvantaged* groups, have completely forgotten that this is a Christian country made up by and large of decent law-abiding people who don't expect and don't want government to solve all their problems."

"That's right," the caller said. "It's about time people woke up to see what's happening. Just the other day I stood in line at the store behind this black woman paying for her groceries with food stamps. What really got me…she bought all kinds of fancy stuff like imported cheese, filet mignon, and some of those fancy bottles of water that come all the way from France. I mean, where's the justice? Here I am buying third-grade hamburger and chicken wings and this lady is eating better than I am."

"I hear you and I sympathize with your frustration," Brewster said. "Your description of what you saw at the market speaks volumes, because that's happening all over the country. I'd bet my mother's pension the woman you describe is probably on welfare. Wake up, America. The welfare system that has been shoved down our throats is going to be the ruination of our country."

"Well, everyone knows it's mostly minorities who are on welfare, and half—if not most of them—could get jobs if they really wanted to," the caller said.

"But why should they?" Brewster's words dripped sarcasm. "Good ole Uncle Sam is there to take care of them. You know that, they know that, we all know that. You've hit on a particularly sore point with me because I am of the old sink or swim school of thinking. If you took welfare away from most of these disadvantaged minorities, they'd have to fend for themselves. It's as simple as that. This may sound a little harsh to some liberals that may be listening. But you know what? I don't care, because I know I'm speaking for most good people in our country…and you can take that to the bank."

Brewster took a quick commercial break and came back a few seconds later to take a new call. "You're on the air," he said.

There was dead silence.

"Caller, go ahead, you're on the air."

"How'd you like the pictures?" the caller said in a deep, muffled voice. He hung up abruptly.

"Probably some liberal who got cold feet at the last moment," Brewster said with a chuckle.

Brewster hadn't opened a sealed brown envelope marked *personal and confidential* that had been delivered to him earlier in the day. It lay on the console in front of him, along with some other pieces of mail.

During a break, he picked it up and pulled out two photographs of a dark-skinned man and a white woman having sex. An attached typewritten note attached said: *See any family resemblance? You'll be hearing from me soon.* Brewster was puzzled. Probably a nut, he thought as he flipped the switch to go back on the air.

The next day Brewster had almost forgotten about the photographs. He got a lot of hate mail, which he usually looked at only briefly and threw into the trash. The way he saw it, it meant only one thing. He was getting to *them*, the liberals, and he loved it.

Brewster sat at home watching a TV game show when the phone rang.

"How'd you like the pictures?" said a man with a deep, southern drawl.

"Who is this?"

"How'd you like the pictures?" the caller insisted.

"I don't know what you're talking about. You got the wrong number."

"They're your mama and daddy. I've got proof that your father was a black man, Mister Brewster. The pictures are only part of that proof. Now listen closely. I want ten thousand dollars in small bills and I'll be out of town and out of your life."

"I don't have to listen to you. This is blackmail. I'm calling the police."

"Go right ahead, and I promise you that by tomorrow morning there'll be a juicy story in the newspaper telling the whole sordid story about where you came from. I know a couple of *liberal* reporters who would just love to print the story—whether or not it's true, which it is. The choice is yours. You have exactly twenty-four hours to make up your mind."

"Wait...how can I reach you?" Brewster asked.

"I'll call you again. Just don't do anything stupid, or I swear I'll do what I said." He hung up.

Brewster wondered if maybe somebody was trying to set him up. But who? And why?

The pictures. He had forgotten all about them. He had put them in his briefcase and brought them home and then...the trash can. They were in with the garbage he'd put out yesterday afternoon. He dashed out the front door and saw the bag of garbage still sitting in a container at the edge of his driveway.

It took him less than a minute to sift through the trash and pull out the brown envelope. Later, after he had examined the photographs and the note that came with them, he called his agent, Mel Ryan, and told him he needed to see him…right away. "About a very delicate matter," he emphasized.

"Let's look at this from the devil's perspective, so to speak," Mel said, getting up from the couch to freshen his drink. "Is there any possibility that what the caller said is true?"

"Of course not." Brewster followed Mel and picked up a bottle of beer he had already started.

"No offense, but how do you really know where you came from? I mean, I know you were adopted. Maybe…"

"My adoptive parents were Florida crackers, for God's sake. You think they would have adopted me if I were anything *but* white? I'm telling you, the whole thing's a scam."

Mel took a sip of his drink. "For the sake of argument, is there any evidence—documents, letters, a birth certificate, that kind of thing—that we can use to refute his allegations? I mean, if it ever comes to that?"

"I have a birth certificate, that's all. You know how secretive most adoptive agencies were back in the sixties."

"What about your adoptive parents? Didn't they ever tell you anything? Anything at all?"

Brewster shook his head. "Once when I thought I might want to find my birth parents, I asked them a few questions, but they didn't seem to know much."

"The way I see it," Mel said, frowning, "you have two choices. You can go to the police—which I wouldn't advise—or you can pay him. I don't have to tell you what this kind of story, as bogus as it may be, would do to your career. You don't need this kind of publicity, not when New York is just around the corner. You have a shot at hosting your own national radio show. I'd hate to see you blow it."

"So what are you saying?"

"I'm saying you have to look out for number one, and if that means paying somebody off, well…"

"You're not serious, are you?"

"This would only be a temporary thing," Mel explained. "After we negotiate the New York contract, we'll figure out a better plan."

Brewster picked up one of the photographs and stared at it for a moment. Then he looked up at Mel. "Okay, let's do it."

"It's the only way." Mel put down his drink and walked toward the door. "Call me when it's done and we'll figure out the next step."

The payoff went off without a hitch—ten thousand dollars in small bills dropped into a garbage can behind a Chinese bakery, just like he was told to do. He had bought some time, and that was all that mattered.

Eleven

Kate Guadagno looked the part—a spoiled rich man's wife, with too much money and all the time in the world to spend it. As she did twice a week, Mondays and Fridays, she went to the upscale stores at Bal Harbour, sometimes to shop, but usually to browse, eat lunch, and be seen. That day, Friday, she finished early and left the stores with a single bagful of goods.

She had neared her car when she spotted a plain white envelope tucked behind the wipers. Curious, she stepped forward and reached to remove it. When she opened it and saw what it contained, she gave out a quick gasp.

Your real mom and dad enjoying themselves, said the note taped to a photograph. She quickly closed the envelope and stuffed it into her purse.

"Just calm down and take a sip of your wine," said her husband, Sal. "It was probably some harmless sicko who gets a kick out of doing this kind of thing." He poured her more wine, then got up and went to the bedroom to make a phone call.

"Listen up," he said, speaking slowly. "Some creep put a porno picture on my wife's car and she's pretty upset about it. I want you to take a couple of the boys and stay close to her, to make sure she's not bothered. You know? If you see anyone around her that looks like he's up to something, grab the son of a bitch and bring him to me."

"How long do we stay with her?" asked the voice on the other end.

"Until I tell you different."

"Sure, boss, whatever you say."

Sal returned to the living room and sat back down on the couch, next to Kate.

"Whoever did it *knew* I was adopted," Kate said. "Don't you see? That's why he left the note."

"How could he know such a thing? And what's the big deal, anyway?"

"The big deal is that the man in the picture had very dark skin," she said, almost shouting.

"I think you're making too much out of this. If you ask me, the guy's a fucking psycho. They get their jollies by doing this kind of thing. I'll bet he waited somewhere close, watching your reaction and jerking himself off at the same time. That's what they do, these sick bastards, 'cause they can't get it up any other way."

Kate gulped her wine. "Maybe you're right. Maybe I am making too much out of this."

Sal got up slowly and paused for a moment. "Trust me, this guy, whoever he is, is not going to bother you again. That, you can be sure of. Now that this little crisis is over, I've got to get back to work." He leaned over to give her a quick kiss, then left the house.

A half hour passed. Kate was in the middle of drawing a bath when she heard the phone ring. It rang six times, stopped, and rang again. She hesitated for a second, then ran to answer it.

"Hello?"

"For a moment I thought you weren't going to answer," said a man with deep voice. "Listen carefully. I've got more pictures and I can prove your real daddy was black. This is no joke, lady. If you're as smart as I think you are, you'll do as I say."

"Why are you doing this to me?"

"It's very simple. I want ten thousand dollars in cash and

you'll never hear from me again. I'm sure a rich, pretty woman like yourself wouldn't want people to know that she happens to be part black. Think about it. Your high society friends, the very white country club you belong to, and even your husband...Sal's his name, isn't it? What's it going to do to him? Have I made my point?"

She took a breath and tried to collect herself. "You say you know about my parents. How do I know you're telling the truth?"

"I wouldn't make up a thing like that. Besides, it's all documented and there are people in Miami who know the whole story."

"What people?"

"It's not important. All you have to know is that I'm prepared to send packages of photographs and information about you to certain people all over town. It's up to you, pretty lady."

"What...do I have to do?"

"Good. We're getting somewhere." He gave her specific instructions about when and where to deliver the money and before hanging up, he gave his usual warning about not calling the police.

It didn't take long for Sal to get home after getting Kate's phone call. The first thing he did after he walked in the door was go to the closet in the den where he kept the equipment that recorded all phone calls. His insurance, he liked to say, in case he ever had to go to the Feds for protection. He played back the caller's call and made a mental note of the things he said. After that, he went into the living room and joined his wife.

"Everything's going to be okay," he said as he reached to pour her a drink.

"I don't need a drink," Kate snapped. She knew about his equipment and waited for him to say something, but he just looked at her as if he were still playing the tape over in his mind. "Well, do you think what he said could be true?" she asked. "About my natural father being black?"

"Who knows?" he said with a shrug. "Who cares? Is that the only thing bothering you?"

She crossed her arms and looked down for second. "If it *did* turn out to be true, would it change anything between us? I mean, I know how you feel about…"

"Look at this," he said, comparing his dark, Sicilian skin with Kate's warm honey complexion. "Hell, I'm darker than you are. My sister Asunta was so dark we used to joke that maybe Papa had nailed one of the black maids while Mama was away." He chuckled. "And another thing. The last time I saw a map of the world, Sicily, where my family originally came from, looks awfully close to Africa. Need I say more?"

She looked at him and smiled. "Thanks, Sal. I knew I could count on you. Maybe I will have that drink after all. Want to join me?"

Sal poured her a gin and soda and looked at his watch. "Some guys are waiting for me," he said as he got up to leave. "I really have to run."

He was almost at the door when she called out to him, "Sure you won't change your mind?" She had removed her blouse and started to take off her bra.

He thought about it for a second and then made his way back to the couch. "Let 'em wait," he said with a grin.

Kate followed the blackmailer's instructions and drove to Little Havana, where she dropped the bagful of money into a dumpster behind a small grocery store. She left the area quickly, without looking back.

Within minutes, a man dressed in a pizza delivery uniform drove up, got out of his car, and retrieved the bag. He lifted a leg to get back in his car when two men came from around the side of the store and grabbed him.

"Don't give us a hard time," one of them said as they hustled him into a car that had pulled up beside them. They closed the doors and sped away.

"What are you doing?" the pizza man shouted. "Who are you, anyway?"

"Just shut up until we get where we're going," one of the men said to him.

"Look, I don't know who you think I am, but I was just…"

"He told you to shut the fuck up," the second man said, producing a 9mm pistol. He jammed it up to the man's throat and held it there for a few seconds. "I don't want any trouble from you. Do you understand?"

The man's eyes widened and he nodded rapidly. He didn't say another word for the rest of the ride. When they got to Sal's house, they took the man into the den and sat him down between the two of them. Sal stood across from them, eyeing the man's uniform.

"What the hell is this?"

"Can someone please tell me what's going on?" the pizza man asked. "Why have you brought me here?"

"Cut the crap," Sal said. "You put that porno picture on my wife's car and you called her on the phone." He said it as if he really didn't believe it. The voice on the phone sounded different, deeper, as he recalled.

"Look, I don't know what you're talking about. I deliver pizzas, is what I do. I was on my way to deliver a pizza when these two guys kidnapped me and brought me here. Honest to God, I'm telling the truth."

"You were delivering a pizza to the back of a grocery store?" Sal said. "Are you trying to fuck with me?"

"No, no," he said, shaking his head. "You see, this guy called and ordered a pizza, double cheese, pepperoni and onions, and then he asked me to do him a favor. He said he'd pay me an extra twenty and so I said I'd do it. I thought it was kind of strange, but for twenty bucks, hey, what the hell."

"Who was he? Where does he live?"

"Danny, that's all he gave. He wanted me to deliver the pizza and the bag to a house in Coconut Grove."

"Had you been there before?" Sal asked.

"No, and I'd never taken an order from him before either."

Sal paced the floor and stroked his chin. "Did you look in the bag?" He stared the man in the eye.

"No, honest," the man said, his voice rising. "I just grabbed it and then the next thing, these two guys were around me. I promise I won't tell anybody…I mean, not that I have anything to tell. There must be a way to resolve this. I'll do anything, anything you say."

Sal stepped away to the other side of the room and gestured to one of the men.

"The pizza man doesn't know shit," Sal said, in a half whisper. "The way I see it, this fucking Danny probably hung around near the back of the store, playing it cool. He was probably going to stop the pizza man once he left the area. Why don't you check out the house in the Grove? It's probably bogus, but see what's there anyway."

"What about the pizza man?"

"Give him a hundred-dollar bill and take him back to where you found him. Make sure you let him know that he's getting off easy. Know what I mean?"

After the men left, Kate walked into the den and sat next to Sal, who poured himself a drink.

"Was he the one?" she asked.

Sal shook his head. "Clever son of a bitch. But don't worry. I don't think he'll bother you again."

"You really think that's the end of it?"

Sal paused for a moment and took a sip of his drink. "I don't know. But just in case, I'll have one of the boys be your chauffeur for the next few days."

Ordinarily Kate would have objected, but not this time. She kind of liked being the center of attention in Sal's life, and she let him know it by sharing his drink and snuggling up to him the way she used to before they were married.

Twelve

Sarah's phone call didn't come as a surprise. She was being blackmailed again. Only this time the blackmailer demanded ten thousand dollars and she didn't know what to do. She dialed Coopersmith. They agreed to meet at a bagel bar in North Miami.

"I feared something like this would happen," Coopersmith said. He waited for the waitress to deliver the coffee and bagels, then continued. "I hoped everything would just stay in the past, but I guess it was too much to hope for."

"You discovered something, didn't you? Why didn't you tell me?"

"Look, after you told me to drop the case, a few things happened that made me get back into it…for my own reasons." He filled her in on everything that happened, from the time the phantom driver nearly killed him, to his meeting with the man who tried to blackmail her. He repeated everything Morrison told him and when he was through, he paused and said with a tinge of regret, "Maybe he and his wife would still be alive if I hadn't shown up at his trailer the way I did."

Sarah looked away for a moment to wipe away the tears from her eyes. She hadn't expected to learn so much about where she came from and she said in a quiet, wistful way, "All my illusions are gone. I'll never have the joy of hugging my mother and telling her that it didn't matter why she had to give me up." She took a deep breath and turned back to Coopersmith. "Did the man say where the rest of Rebecca's children might be? What about Amos? What happened to him?"

Coopersmith produced a folder and placed it on top of the table. "It's all here. Morrison's notes and papers. He gave them to me after he unburdened himself."

"You've had this information and you didn't call me?"

"I was off the case, remember? Anyway, I never bothered to look through any of it. As far as I was concerned, Morrison's secrets belonged in the past. In a way, I wished he hadn't given them to me." He pushed the folder closer to Sarah. "Go ahead. See what's in there. There may be a clue or two about the guy who's blackmailing you now. One of the last things Morrison said to me was that he kept a duplicate folder. It was stolen from a locked cabinet in an office he used to have before his wife got sick."

Sarah hesitated, then opened the folder and pulled out some papers. "It looks like Morrison kept a record of every adoption. Names, dates, addresses, money paid…it's all here."

Coopersmith picked up a couple of sheets, glanced through them, and put them aside. Then he reached into the folder and pulled out a bulging envelope with a rubber band tied around it. He removed the rubber band, looked inside, and quickly closed it. "I'll hold on to these," he said. They were pictures of Rebecca and Amos having sex.

Sarah didn't say anything. Her eyes were fixed on the page that contained information about herself. Her parents had paid four thousand dollars plus a one hundred dollar fee for a fake birth certificate. She flipped through some more pages and found some information about Daniel, the only baby for which Morrison didn't receive any money. They placed him with a childless black couple named Edna and Billy Griffin from Overtown.

Sarah looked up at Coopersmith. "I want to find them, all of them—my father, my brothers and sister. Can you help me?"

Coopersmith frowned, slightly. "You're not serious, are you? They may not be as open-minded as you about being told they're part black."

"I can't worry about it. Now that I know my mother is dead, it's important for me to find them."

"Have you forgotten about the blackmailer?"

"No, but the way I see it, he's out of luck. When I hear from him again, I'll tell him so. He can go ahead and tell whoever he wants. I don't care."

"What about your husband?"

"Things are different, now that I know the whole story. He doesn't know about the recent blackmail demand, but I'm going to tell him about it and I'm also going to tell him I want to find my natural family. If he can't accept it, well…"

"It's none of my business, but you may want to think it over. Like I said once before, some things are better left alone."

"But they're my family," she said, her voice rising. "I just know I'll never have any peace until I find them. I really would appreciate it if you would help me."

Coopersmith waited a few seconds and then gave a weak smile. "I'll start tomorrow, if it's soon enough for you."

Sarah smiled back. "I promise you this time, I won't tell you to back off…for any reason. By the way, what was in that envelope?"

"Pictures. They're not the kind you'd want in your family album. I'll dispose of them when I get back to my office."

Sarah nodded. "Well, I guess that's it." She paused for a moment, then got up to leave. "Call me when you find something."

Coopersmith stayed behind to finish his bagel and a second cup of coffee. He took his time reading through Morrison's papers and made a mental note of all the things he had to do. For starters, he had to call a good research specialist like his old Bureau buddy, Ray Difalco from Jacksonville, to get an update on all the names and addresses. If he were lucky, it wouldn't be too difficult unless the people had died or moved around a lot.

Thirteen

"For Christ's sake, don't tell me any more stories or I'll bust a gut." Coopersmith laughed into the mouthpiece.

"That reminds me," Difalco said. "Do you remember Miss Shoemaker's special plant? The one she kept on top of her desk?"

"Yeah, I remember. She used to talk to it like it was a person. Even gave it a name. Miss Grady, I think she called it. She couldn't figure out why it turned yellow and shriveled up. Don't tell me you had something to do with that?"

Difalco chuckled. "Let's just say we used to get real bored working the midnight-to-eight shift. Actually, it was Dave's doing. You remember Dave, don't you? Went on to become an agent in Phoenix. I heard he later became assistant special agent in charge. Anyway, one night Dave sat at Miss Shoemaker's desk and he kept looking at the plant. You know how much he hated Miss Shoemaker. For years she'd been threatening to fire him if he didn't shape up. Well, next thing he does, he takes the plant into the bathroom and a couple of minutes later comes back out smiling like a Cheshire cat. He'd taken a leak right into the fucking plant." Difalco broke into uncontrollable laughter. "Just watering the plant, he says real cool like. Then he puts it back on the desk. For four days in a row he *watered* it until it finally dried up and died."

Coopersmith laughed even harder and had to force himself

to calm down. "No more stories, please," he said, pleading. "You ought to put them in a book. I'm serious. You'd probably make a fortune." He cleared his throat and then brought up the reason for his phone call. He gave Difalco a rundown on Sarah's case and requested he check every data bank from Florida to California. "I'm counting on your bloodhound instincts to bring everything up-to-date."

"Speaking of bloodhounds, did I ever tell you about the stray dog that snuck into the building one night?"

Coopersmith hesitated. "No, but do me favor. Write it down and put it with the information you're sending me."

"Hey, that's not a bad idea. I can send a copy to all the guys we used to work with."

Coopersmith still had a smile on his face after hanging up the phone. If he hadn't said good-bye, Difalco could have talked for hours, telling one hilarious story after another. Not that he minded. At almost noon he had to meet his sister-in-law for lunch at a place called the Taj Mahal just north of Hialeah. It was on the other side of town and he'd have to hustle to make it there on time.

"So how's your love life?" Laura asked.

"This vindaloo sauce is pretty good," Coopersmith said. "Didn't think I'd like it. Kind of reminds me of that Mexican sauce. You know, the one that has chocolate in it."

"You're evading the question." She flashed a broad smile.

"So who has time for a love life? I work all day long, nights, weekends. After Maria died, I just worked even harder and I guess I haven't found a reason to slow down."

"It's been five years, Joe. Maria was my sister and I miss her very much. But I think it's time to move on."

He put down his fork and took a sip of his water. "Look, I know what you're trying to do and I appreciate your concern. But…I don't know how to say this. I'm not as lonely as you think I am and the reason is that I'm happy with my memories of Maria. It's as simple as that. I'm okay, really I am. So stop worrying about me." He picked up his fork again. "So tell me about the kids. I haven't seen them in…"

"In over six months," Laura said.

"Has it been that long?"

"It's been that long." She nodded. "We'll have to do something about that. Why don't you come for dinner tomorrow night? Bill and the kids would love to see you."

"Thanks, but I've just taken on a big case and…"

"We'll expect you at seven. One of the last things Maria said to me was 'Take care of the big lug,' and that's exactly what I'm doing."

"Okay, okay, I'll be there," he said with a quick smile. "I'll bring dessert."

After reviewing Difalco's preliminary report, Coopersmith called Sarah at home and got no answer. He left a message on her recorder to call him, which she did a half hour later.

"I got your message." He heard the tension in her voice.

"What's the matter?"

"He called…just a few minutes ago. He came right out with it and told that me that if I didn't pay him the ten thousand dollars, he'd mail out packages of photographs and information to certain people."

"What did you tell him?"

"I told him to go right ahead, that I knew about my parents and about how I was adopted. I threw in a few tidbits from Morrison's report just to let him know that I knew as much as he did."

"What did he say?"

"Nothing. I think I took the wind out of his sails and I guess he didn't know what to say. Finally he mumbled something and then hung up." She sighed. "I don't know why, but I'm suddenly having mixed emotions about all of this."

"Because of the phone call?"

"No…well, partly. What I mean is that I'm a little afraid. It's hard to explain. But I'll be all right. So, tell me about Difalco's report."

"Well, he came up with some good leads. I'm taking a flight to Atlanta tomorrow morning to look for your brother, Hal Brewster. If everything goes right, I should be back the same night or the following morning." He paused. "It's still not too late to back out of this, you know."

She thought about it for a second. "You're going to talk your way out of a job if you keep that up," she said lightheartedly. "Just go out and find my family and bring me back some good news."

When Coopersmith arrived in Atlanta, he had Brewster's entire credit history for the past seven years. More important, he had his current address, in a quiet middle-class neighborhood.

At almost 11:00 a.m. he drove up to Brewster's house, got out of his car, and walked up to the door. He rang the bell, but there was no answer. Brewster's car sat in the middle of the driveway, so he knew someone was home, probably watching out a window. He rang the bell a couple more times and followed it with a knock. Slowly the door opened.

"Jesus, can't a man have a little peace and quiet?" Brewster looked as if he'd just gotten out of bed. He wore his pajamas which fit snugly over his portly build. "You'd better not be a salesman, or I'll..."

"I'm not a salesman, Mister Brewster. I'm Joe Coopersmith, a private investigator from Miami. I'd like to speak to you about...a rather important matter. May I come in?"

Brewster hesitated. "All right, come in. I work the late shift at the station and sometimes I don't get home 'til two or three in the morning. If you hadn't pounded on my door, I'd still be cutting Zs. Why don't you take a seat while I get my coffee?" He disappeared into the kitchen and came back holding a mug with a happy face painted on its side.

"So, what can I do for you?" Brewster sat across the room.

"Well, first of all, I want you to know that what I'm about to tell you may sound a little strange, but I assure you it's all true. You see, the person who hired me is a woman who was adopted as an infant. She knew nothing about her birth parents or whether she had brothers and sisters—until recently. It turns out her mother was deceased and she does in fact have siblings. Which brings me to the reason I'm here. Mister Brewster, I have reason to believe you are her brother."

"I have a sister?" Brewster asked in disbelief. "What's her name?"

"Sarah, Sarah Baker. My job was to locate you and find out if you would be willing to meet her."

"I don't know what to say. I've always known I was adopted, but I never gave it much thought. If what you say is true, of course I want to meet her. What about the others?"

"You have another sister whom I haven't found, and of course Sarah, who lives in Miami. There's a fourth sibling, a brother, but I don't know much about him."

"You obviously know a lot about my family. What about our father? Where is he?"

"I don't know," Coopersmith said, shaking his head. "I'm still working on it. But there is something I *do* know about him."

"What are you talking about?"

Coopersmith cleared his throat. "Your father was black. It's a long story, but when you and the others were adopted, both of your parents were listed as white and no one ever…"

"Wait a minute," Brewster said, standing up. "Did someone send you here for more money? Is that what this is about? Get the hell out of here or I'm calling the police."

Coopersmith got up and tried to calm him down. "I think I know what's going on here. If you'll give me a minute, I can explain everything. You probably got a letter from someone trying to blackmail you, didn't you? He did it with Sarah, too. Don't you see what he's trying to do?"

Brewster didn't want to listen, and rushed Coopersmith to

the door. "Just leave me alone," he shouted, slamming the door behind him.

Coopersmith took the next plane back to Miami. He called Sarah later that evening and told her about Brewster, and how the blackmailer had already gotten to him. She took the news well, though she worried the blackmailer would get to her sister, if he hadn't already.

"Where the hell have you been?" Brewster screeched into his car phone. "I've been trying to reach you for hours."

"I went to my cousin's wedding in Macon," Mel said. "I thought I told you about it"

"Never mind. Just listen. This guy dropped by my house claiming to be a private investigator from Miami. His client is a woman who is searching for her siblings. At first I thought, great. I have a sister. But then he dropped this bit about my father being black and I just knew I was being set up all over again."

"Could you tell if it was the same guy who called you?"

"I don't know and I didn't want to find out. I told him to leave. What am I going to do, Mel? If this thing turns out to be true, my whole career will go down the tubes."

"Let me think about it. In the meantime, don't tell anyone, and for God's sake don't panic. If the private investigator calls again, just listen to him and find out as much as you can."

"Okay, Mel. I'll...I'll do that." He stared at the road ahead. "Maybe this thing will blow over, don't you think?"

Mel didn't answer for a couple of seconds. "I don't know. I have to figure this out before it gets out of hand. Why don't we meet tomorrow at your place, say around noon, and you can tell me exactly what this guy said to you."

"I'll be waiting for you." Brewster hung up the phone and floored the gas to make the yellow light just ahead.

Fourteen

The next day Coopersmith dropped by his office to pick up the mail and check his incoming faxes. He was in luck. Difalco had come up with information about another sibling, a sister named Kate Guadagno, who lived in Miami Beach. The fax ended with another one of Difalco's stories.

On his way to Kate Guadagno's house on Pine Tree Drive, Coopersmith didn't know what he'd find when he got there. So far he batted zero, and he was halfway expecting she'd slam the door on him the minute he mentioned the reason for his visit. To his surprise, she turned out to be different, in a pleasant kind of way.

Kate smiled. "Tell me all about her."

"To tell you the truth, I don't know her that well. But I suspect the two of you are going to hit it off just fine." He cocked his head to one side, trying to study her. "You know, I just noticed something. You have the same eyes, very expressive. You're sisters all right."

"So when can I meet her?"

"As soon as I talk to Sarah." He got up to leave and hesitated. "Just so there's no misunderstanding, you're not going to change your mind, are you? I mean, this thing about your father and the rest of it…well, you know what I'm trying to say."

"No way am I changing my mind," she said, getting up to see him to the door. "Besides, who cares about the past? Certainly not my husband, Sal. I've always wanted a sister and I'm not going to let anything or anyone spoil it for me. Does that answer your question?"

He smiled. "Sure does."

They were approaching the front door when she heard Sal's car pulling into the garage. "Oh, good. Sal's here and you can meet him."

When Sal stepped in the hallway, Kate reached out to give him a kiss and quickly introduced him to Coopersmith. "He's a private investigator hired to track me down. You're not going to believe this, but I have a sister and she wants to meet me. Isn't that great?"

"Whoa, whoa," Sal said with a wary look in his eye. "What do you mean he was hired to track you down?"

"If I can explain…" Coopersmith offered.

"You can explain nothing," Sal said, "except where I've heard your name before. Were you a cop?"

"No, I worked for the FBI."

"I knew I heard that name before. Look, pal, maybe you're on the level, maybe you're not. But until I know for sure, why don't you take a hike and forget you ever came here."

Kate put her hands on her hips. "But Sal, I already told him…"

"I don't care what you said to him." He shot her a look that told her he'd talk to her later.

"I guess I'll be on my way," Coopersmith said, walking out the door. "If you change your mind, Kate, you know where to reach me."

"What the hell's going on?" Sal said the moment Coopersmith left the house. "I come in here and I see you standing next to this schmuck that I don't know from Adam and then you start talking shit to me about having a sister. Did it occur to you that maybe he was trying to con you just like the guy who sent you the picture?"

"My mind doesn't work that way." Kate retreated into the living room. "Besides, he didn't want anything from me. He came to deliver a message from a sister that I never knew existed. What's the big deal?"

He shook his head, exasperated. "The big deal is that we don't know anything about him or your sister—if there really is a sister."

"Will it make you feel better if I told you Coopersmith knows about the guy with the pictures? He doesn't know who he is, but he said the guy tried the same thing with Sarah—that's my sister's name."

Sal shook his head again. "You don't get it, do you? First some asshole sends you the picture, and then this private eye shows up a few days later. Something's going on here that smells as bad as a piece of old provolone."

"So what do you want me to do?" Her voice cracked. "Forget that I have a sister who's been trying to find me? You're not being fair, Sal." She turned her back on him so he wouldn't see the tears in her eyes.

"Okay," he said after a few seconds. "If it means that much to you, I'll tell you what I'm going to do. I'll check Coopersmith out and your sister, too, and if everything comes out okay, then..."

"You're the best, Sal." she turned around and put her arms around him.

He smiled. He would milk this for all it was worth. "About that massage you've been promising..." He removed his coat.

After leaving Kate's house, Coopersmith called Sarah and gave her the old good news/bad news routine about his meeting with Kate. Sarah heard only what she wanted to hear and urged him to give it another try.

"Unless my gut feeling is wrong, I'd say I won't have to," Coopersmith said. "Somehow or another, Kate is going to get around her husband on this, maybe even sooner than expected."

"You really think so?"

"My guess is, she's going to call before the end of the week. And when she does...well, my job is over, at least with this one."

Coopersmith was right. Two days later, Kate called, ready to meet Sarah. What she didn't say was that she did it behind Sal's back.

To Coopersmith, it was enough that she called, and he quickly called Sarah to let her know. "You should be hearing from her any moment. Good luck…not that you'll need it. I mean, there's no need to get nervous or anything. Well, you know what I'm trying to say."

"Thanks, Mister Coopersmith. I'll let you know what happens."

Fifteen

Sitting at a picnic table off the 79th Street Causeway, Sarah's mind wandered, and more than once she had to apologize for not being more attentive.

"It's understandable," Coopersmith said. "I had already figured that your husband wasn't too thrilled about your new-found sister. And I can just imagine what he'll say when he hears about your brother, Daniel. You may even want to reconsider this one."

"Why?" she shot back. "Because he's the dark one?"

"Because he's serving a three-year sentence at Marianna."

"What's he there for?"

"White-collar crime. Something to do with a mail order scam."

Sarah got up from the table and walked over to the water's edge. Coopersmith joined her. "Sure looks nice out there. Almost makes me wish I had a boat."

"Somehow I can't picture you enjoying yourself in anything that floats." Sarah smiled.

"You pegged me right. I love the water, always have, but only from a distance, like from my fifth-story balcony."

"Look, Mister Coopersmith," she said, her smile fading. "I've got to finish what I started. I don't care that Daniel's in prison. I want you to talk to him and find out as much as you can."

"You sure about this?"

"No...but he's the last of the siblings, and I'm not letting my personal problems get in the way of finishing what I started. Not after we've come this far."

They ambled back to the table and talked some more, mostly about Kate and how well she and Sarah were getting along. When Coopersmith said he had to leave for another appointment, Sarah decided to stay.

"I need to clear my mind for a while longer." She gazed out into the bay. "Call me the moment you get back. If you can't reach me at home, try Dolores's number. She doesn't know it yet, but she's about to have a roommate."

Coopersmith tried not to act surprised. "I understand." He tipped his head and strolled away.

Arriving in Tallahassee the next morning, Coopersmith rented a car, stopped for a quick bagel and coffee, and drove west to Marianna. He got there an hour later, just as a young woman and her freckled-faced little boy riding in a white compact pulled up beside him. He recognized them from the plane and he smiled at them.

"We're going to see Daddy," the little boy shouted as they stepped out of the car.

Coopersmith followed them into the reception building and took a seat in a large waiting room. The boy's mother looked distressed, as though she really didn't want to be there. She glanced at her watch every so often and alternately puffed on a cigarette, her second in less than twenty minutes.

"I hate this waiting," she said. "I've never understood why it takes so long. Do you come here often?"

"This is my third time in two years."

"My son and I try to come up every month. We used to drive, but it just took too much out of me." She paused to crush her cigarette in an ashtray. "I do it mostly for him. He really loves his daddy."

"He seems to take it pretty well." Coopersmith observed the

boy entertaining himself with a box of crayons and a coloring book.

"A lot better than me, that's for sure. Ever since my husband got arrested, things have just gone from bad to worse. I've had two jobs in the past five months, and just before coming here, my boss called and told me not to bother coming to work anymore. Something about downsizing the workforce, he said, whatever that meant. You wouldn't know of a good job back in Miami, would you?" She shook her head. "Never mind, I don't even know you and I'm bothering you with my problems."

"That's all right. As a matter of fact, I do run into some good prospects now and then." He reached into his wallet, pulled out a business card, and handed it to her. "I can't promise anything, but you can call me if you want. It's up to you."

"Thanks." She read the card and looked up at him. "You're a private investigator? I've never met one before. You must be here on business, or can't you say?"

Coopersmith was about to answer when he heard the little boy suddenly shout across the room, "It's Daddy. It's Daddy!" The boy's father entered the room; the boy raced up and gave him a hug.

"How about Mommy," the father said, turning to his wife standing off to one side. "Isn't she going to give Daddy a hug?"

The mother forced a smile and hugged her husband in a way that let him know she only did it for the benefit of their son. "How you doing, Johnny?" They sat at a table next to a vending machine.

When Daniel entered the lounge five minutes later, Coopersmith got up and paused for a moment. He had expected him to look different, more stereotypically black. Daniel had a thin, dark face with semi-fine features and a shock of straight, black hair combed to the back. Coopersmith walked up and introduced himself, then led the way to the corner of the room, where they took a seat.

"My client's name is Sarah Baker," Coopersmith began. "I

know the name doesn't mean anything to you, but as you'll soon see, there are…"

"You came to tell me she's my sister," he said with a bit of smugness in his voice. "And she's being blackmailed."

Coopersmith stared at him. "How did you know?"

"Does it matter?"

"After talking to the others, your brother and sister, I was just curious, that's all."

"So now that you've found me. What next? A brother sister reunion?" Daniel laughed and shook his head.

"Well, as a matter of fact, that's exactly what she wants to do. She's a very down-to-earth lady who's trying very hard to come to terms with her past." He looked at Daniel carefully. There was something familiar about him, something he couldn't quite put his finger on. "She wants to get to know you and she doesn't care about…"

"About my being black?" Daniel said, raising an eyebrow. "How very big of her."

"I was going to say about you being in this place. Look, all I need to know is whether you'd welcome a phone call, a letter, or whatever from her. If the answer is no, I'll go back to Miami and tell her it didn't work out. If the answer is yes, then my job is over and the two of you can communicate however you want."

Daniel crossed his arms, then stroked his chin thoughtfully. "You seem like a decent man, Mister Coopersmith, but I really don't know you and I'm not sure how to answer your questions."

"What are you saying?"

"Well, you probably know about Morrison and his file, otherwise you wouldn't know about me."

Coopersmith nodded. "It's all falling into place. I had a hunch you were the one who broke into his office and stole his file."

"If you figured that out, then you'll probably figure out the rest."

"The rest?"

"About the blackmailer." Daniel looked around as if to make sure nobody was listening. He leaned closer. "I really shouldn't be telling you this, but somebody's got to stop him. Until now I didn't know who to tell, so in a way I'm glad you came to see me. The truth is, I feel responsible for what's happening. It all started when I tried to do the same thing as Sarah, search for my roots and all that. That was after my parents told me about my adoption and about Morrison, who used to do legal work for them and other black families in Overtown. The first thing I did was find Morrison, which was easy. But I knew he'd never admit to anything, much less agree to help me find my birth parents. That's why I broke into his office, to see what I could find."

"And you got lucky."

"That's right. I had heard he was a crotchety old eccentric, the kind who holds on to things forever. Anyway, after I read the file and learned that my birth mother was dead, I basically put the matter out of my mind. Unlike Sarah, I had no interest in meeting my brother and sisters or even my father."

"Did you tell anyone about what the file contained?"

Daniel nodded and again leaned forward. "Shortly after I got here, I became friends with this white guy, Steve Anderson, who was into computers almost as much as me. I got to know him pretty well, and one day I happened to mention that I was adopted. I also told him about the information in Morrison's file. At the time I didn't see any harm in it. But then, right before his release, he asked where I kept the file, and I very stupidly told him it was in a locked briefcase with my parents in Miami." He paused and gave out a long sigh. "I wish I'd never said anything to him about it."

"You mean he went to Miami and stole the file from your parents' house?"

"He didn't exactly steal it. The guy was smooth, real smooth. He told my mom that I had sent him to pick up the briefcase for some kind of project he and I were working on. My mom's a very trusting person, and she gave it to him. I don't blame her, but I wish she had talked to me about it."

Coopersmith looked up for a moment, not really sure what to make of Daniel and his story about the file. "When did you find out about it, that he had blackmailed your brother and sisters?"

"I didn't. But considering he was in here for running some kind of fraud on the elderly, what else could he be doing with the information? The guy was a professional con man. As soon as you mentioned Sarah's name, I just knew he'd already gotten to her."

"Just so you know, Sarah and your other sister Kate didn't fall for his little blackmail scheme, which brings me back to the reason I came. What do you want me to tell Sarah?"

There was a brief silence. "Tell her I'll need some time to think about it. You may not understand, Mister Coopersmith, but I'm comfortable being black because that's the way I was raised. If I meet Sarah, I think a part of me would want to be something I've never been."

Coopersmith nodded. "What about your father? Would you want to see him?"

"I think I would want to meet him," Daniel said after considering it for a long moment. "Have you found him?"

"Not yet. No one seems to know what happened to him. My associate has checked every data system in the country and can't find a single trace on him. It's like he fell into a dark hole. I'm not giving up though, at least not unless Sarah decides to end the investigation."

"What about Steve? What are you going to do about him?"

"Well, there's not much I can do. Your brother Hal wasn't exactly thrilled to see me, which means he probably paid Steve to keep quiet about the contents of the file. I wouldn't feel too sorry for him, though."

"Why is that?"

Coopersmith shrugged. "Let's just say you're better off not knowing him. By the way, when is your release date?"

"I'm up for a parole hearing. If I get it, I should be out in a few weeks."

Coopersmith gave him his business card, then got up and shook his hand. "When you've made up your mind about meeting Sarah, give me a call."

On his way back to the airport, Coopersmith thought about Daniel and his reason for not wanting to meet Sarah just yet. Maybe he was right. Maybe if he did meet her, a part of him would want to be something he could never be. White. For Daniel's sake, he hoped he'd never hear from him.

When Coopersmith arrived in Miami, he called Sarah but she didn't answer. He tried Dolores's house, where he found her and spoke to her briefly.

"I'm spending the next few days here," she said. "Would you mind coming over?"

"I think the two of you know each other," Sarah said as they sat down at the kitchen table. Coopersmith and Dolores exchanged brief pleasantries, then Coopersmith turned to Sarah.

"I had a very interesting conversation with Daniel," Coopersmith said slowly. "He already knew about you and the others."

Sarah and Dolores looked at each other. "How could that be?" Sarah asked. "No one knows about Morrison's file."

"Except the person who stole the original one from his office," Dolores said.

"Very good," Coopersmith said with a smile. "Your detective instincts are still there. To make a long story short, Daniel admitted he had stolen the file trying to find out where he came from. When he read that his mother was dead, he just dropped it and put the file away." Coopersmith repeated everything Daniel had told him, and when he finished, he looked at Sarah. "He's not sure he wants to meet you. He didn't rule it out, though."

"I don't understand," Sarah said. "Is it because he's in prison?"

Coopersmith shook his head. "He feels he can never be a part of your world. He's very astute about this, and he just doesn't want to take any chances."

"What chances? All I want to do is meet him and be a sister to him. Doesn't he know that?"

"The way he sees it, you're white and he's black and there's too much of a gap between the two of you. Basically, he doesn't see a need to bridge that gap, especially since he's comfortable being who he is."

"So what happens next?" Sarah asked.

"Well, he knows how to reach me, so we'll just have to wait and see what he wants to do."

Sarah looked disappointed. "He was the last one and I really hoped I'd get a chance to meet him."

"It may still happen," Coopersmith said.

"By the way, you didn't say whether there was a family resemblance," Sarah said. "What does he look like?"

"He was dark skinned. But his overall features…well, let's just say he doesn't look like your typical black kid from Overtown. He doesn't look anything like you, except for the eyes, maybe. I have to admit that when I first saw him, I…"

"What I don't understand is how this guy, Steve, has been able to get away with trying to blackmail everybody," Dolores interrupted. "Isn't anyone looking into it?"

"I guess not," Coopersmith answered. "Unless a victim comes forward, the cops can't do very much."

"But he's the reason Hal Brewster didn't want to have anything to do with me," Sarah said. "If we can stop him, maybe he'll change his mind."

"It'll take a lot more than that," Coopersmith said. "He made it very clear he didn't want to meet you or any member of your family."

"I think Sarah's right," Dolores said. "If you can find Steve and expose him in some way…"

"And then what? Turn him over to the cops? Do both of you really think this is going to do any good?" He paused to let them think about it. "I'll tell you what I can do. I can have my buddy Difalco check Steve's name through every system from here to California and we'll see what happens."

"Fair enough," Sarah said.

A knock sounded on the door. "We ordered a pizza," Sarah said, getting up to answer it. "It's probably the delivery man. You're welcome to stay and share it with us."

"Thanks, but I really should be going," Coopersmith followed Sarah and waited for her to open the door.

"Mark," Sarah said with a look of surprise. "We were expecting a pizza."

"I need to speak with you," Mark said, his face solemn.

She introduced him to Coopersmith, who shook his hand and quickly left the house.

SIXTEEN

"We've got time for one more caller," Brewster said. He picked up a call from a man who'd been on hold for twenty minutes.

"I heard a rumor the other day," said a muffled-sounding voice on the other end. "This guy who used to live in Miami claimed you were adopted and that you…"

Brewster pressed the dump button and put on a music tape. He let it run until the end of the program, then hastily left the studio.

When he walked in his house a half hour later, he heard the phone ringing and rushed to answer it.

"I had you going there for a moment, didn't I?" the blackmailer said with a chuckle.

"Why are you bothering me? You got your money. If you think you can…"

"Look, I wasn't going to call you, but I've had a few setbacks and I need some cash. Just a couple of grand to tide me over for the next few months."

"Absolutely not. You've gotten all you're getting from me."

"Okay, fine," said the blackmailer, his voice sounding almost friendly. "If that's how you feel, then you leave me no choice. Too bad, though, I kind of liked hearing you on the radio every night. They'll probably replace you with some liberal from up north, maybe even a woman. Wouldn't that be something?" There was a brief pause. "I'll call you back in exactly one hour. Don't disappoint me."

The line went dead. Brewster punched out Mel's number. It rang six times, but he got no answer.

"The son of a bitch is never around when you need him," Brewster muttered, hanging up. "I never should have listened to him in the first place."

Brewster paced the floor, poured himself a drink, and tried calling Mel again. Still no answer. A half hour later, the phone rang. He picked it up on the first ring.

"Break out the champagne," Mel said excitedly. "I just got a call from New York and they want to see you next week. They loved the tapes and they want to make you an offer. I knew it was going to happen but I didn't…"

"There isn't going to *be* a New York," Brewster said.

"What the hell are you talking about?"

"The blackmailer called again and he wants more money. Maybe the private investigator was right. Maybe it's true. I just don't know what to think anymore. All I know is that my career is over. Everything I worked for, everything I planned to do. It's finished and there's nothing I can do about it."

"Get hold of yourself. I told you last time we met to let me do the worrying. Didn't I? We finally got a shot at the big time and believe me, I'm not about to let this thing get in the way."

"But Mel…"

"I didn't want to tell you just yet, but after our last meeting, I contacted someone, a guy they call the Fixer, who knows how to deal with this kind of thing. When he talks to you, just do what he says and don't ask too many questions. In the meantime, go along with the blackmailer, but try to stall him as much as you can."

Brewster hesitated. "I don't know, Mel. Maybe if we go to the police…"

"Forget it. That would be a surefire way of killing whatever chance you have at New York. We're talking the big time—your own limousine, a penthouse apartment. Do you really want to blow it by letting this creep hound you for the rest of your life?"

"Well, when you put it that way, I guess I don't have much choice." Brewster sighed and rubbed his temple. "The guy's supposed to call me back in a few minutes. I'll…do like you said."

"Good. Call me after you talk to him. And don't worry so much. Have I ever steered you wrong before?"

SEVENTEEN

Coopersmith called Difalco early in the morning and gave him Steve Anderson's name. He didn't expect to hear from him for at least a couple of hours, and was surprised when he called ten minutes later.

"Are you trying to test me or something?" Difalco asked.

"What are you talking about?"

"If this guy is your blackmailer, you've got problems. From six feet under it would be awfully hard to do much of anything."

"You mean he's dead? I don't get it. Daniel told me that he had Morrison's file. Are you absolutely sure?"

"The data inquiry came back with one Steve Anderson who was released from Marianna. That's the same guy found beaten to death in a motel room in Mobile, Alabama, about six months ago."

"Anyone arrested?"

"Not yet. From what I can see, it's still an open investigation."

There was a brief silence. "I just thought of something," Coopersmith said. "Mobile is the same town where Sarah's mother is from. I wonder if there's a connection."

"I don't know, but if you want I'll do some research and see what I can find. Before, I mostly focussed on the siblings."

"Good idea. Call me the minute you find something."

After he had hung up, Coopersmith called Sarah at Dolores's

house to make sure she was there and then drove over to see her.

"I've got something on the stove," Sarah said as she led Coopersmith to the kitchen. "It's my therapy. When my dad died last year, I must have cooked enough to feed an army." She stepped up to the stove, stirred the sauce, and turned down the heat to the lowest setting. "You sounded a little mysterious on the phone."

"I got a call from Difalco, the guy running traces on Steve Anderson's name," Coopersmith said. "Are you ready for this? Steve is *dead*, a victim of a homicide in Mobile."

"He was murdered? That means…"

"Right. Whoever killed him is probably the blackmailer."

"This is weird, really weird." Sarah shook her head. "Just thinking about it gives me the creeps. So what are we going to do?"

"The question is, do you really want to pursue it, knowing that your blackmailer may also be a murderer? Personally, I think…"

She grabbed his arm. "You're not quitting on me, are you?"

"I just assumed you'd want to let the cops handle it."

"As far as I'm concerned, this doesn't change a thing. I can't explain it but I have a feeling there's something out there that we've missed." She took a deep breath. "I need closure to my past, and finding the blackmailer may be a way of doing it."

Coopersmith thought about it for a couple of seconds. "If that's what it takes, then I guess I'll just have to find him."

"Good," Sarah said with a wide smile. She got up and stirred the sauce some more. "Have you had lunch yet? I'm making a red wine sauce with portabello mushrooms and sun-dried tomatoes. It's really good over pasta."

"Thanks, but I usually skip lunch. Maybe some other time."

"I'm really a good cook. Just try a little and tell me how you like it." She piled pasta on a plate, ladled the sauce over it, and placed it in front of him.

Coopersmith took a whiff. "Smells great." He picked up a fork and twirled it into the pasta. He tasted a mouthful and looked up at her. "You're right. You *are* a good cook."

Sarah prepared a plate for herself and joined him. She didn't eat much and mostly listened as Coopersmith talked about the case and a possible connection between Sarah's mother's hometown and the murder of Steve Anderson in the same town.

"I've really made a mess of things, haven't I?" she said after a few minutes. "So far I've gained a sister and probably lost a husband. I still love him, you know, and I think he still loves me." She collected the dirty dishes. "Don't mind me. I'm just feeling a little sorry for myself. Maybe I'll cook some more. I've got a Greek cookbook that I brought with me. That should keep my mind occupied for the next few days."

Coopersmith rose to leave. "Thanks for the pasta."

She walked him to the door.

"There's still a chance Daniel will want to meet you. I'll call you if I hear something. In the meantime, keep your fingers crossed."

When Coopersmith returned to his office, he found the woman he had met at Marianna waiting for him in the hallway. She looked like she'd been crying. He opened the door and let her in. "Why don't you have a seat?" He motioned toward the chair in front of his desk. He sat down and waited for her to explain why she'd come.

"I need your help, Mister Coopersmith. They took my boy and they won't give him back. I didn't know who to turn to until I remembered the card you gave me. Is there...a way I can hire you and maybe pay you later after I find a job?"

"Before we get into that, why don't we start from the beginning. Just take your time and tell me what happened."

She nodded and closed her eyes for a moment, collecting herself. "Well, it all started at the prison. After you left, my husband told me that one of his friends had been keeping an eye on me. He thinks I'm cheating on him, which I'm not. Anyway, after me and my boy got back to Miami, I found my husband's parents waiting for me at my apartment. They were awful and called me all kinds of names. They said they were there to pick up my son because according to them they had proof I was an unfit mother."

"What kind of proof?"

"Well, they had a photograph of me talking to this guy on Biscayne Boulevard. They also had another one of the two of us walking into a motel room."

"Are you a hooker?" Coopersmith asked.

"Not exactly," she said without looking at him.

"Not exactly?"

She pursed her lips and waited a moment before answering. "You might as well know that I *used* to be a hooker. During an especially bad period in my life I thought the only thing I had going for me was my body. The first time it happened I felt almost flattered when someone offered me a hundred dollars for doing something I did on an average date. After that I was hooked, if that's the right way to put it. The money was too easy and it got really hard for me to give it up completely."

"I suppose your husband knew about your past."

She nodded. "He was…one of my clients," she said, embarrassed. "I gave up hooking for him and for my boy. That is, until that night when someone took those pictures. I swear to you it was the only time I ever went back to hooking since we got married. I only did it because I was three months behind on the rent and my in-laws refused to help me. They never liked me from the beginning and did everything possible to turn my husband against me."

"Did you call the cops?"

"I thought about it, but they pointed out they were prepared to take me to court if I didn't do as they said. They claimed that my past and the recent photos was enough to prove to a judge that I was unfit to raise Randy. Not having a job didn't help any, and they were going to use that against me as well."

Coopersmith leaned back. "It seems to me that what you need is a lawyer. From what you tell me, these in-laws of yours are not going to give in that easily."

"I can't afford a lawyer, Mister Coopersmith. My only experience with them is that they want cash up front before they even speak to you. If you ask me, they're no better than the hookers on the Boulevard."

Coopersmith stifled an involuntary chuckle. "Well, they're not all that bad. In fact, I know someone who may be interested in taking your case. He's a little strange—still wears clip-on ties, forgets to comb his hair half the time. But he's a good lawyer and he does a lot of pro bono work."

"If pro bono means free, then that's my kind of lawyer," she said with a forced smile.

"You may want to think it over. He's an advocate for prostitutes. Victims of a degenerate society, he likes to say. The downside is that he loves to use the media and there's a good chance your name and face will appear on the six o'clock news."

She shrugged. "I don't think I have much choice. I'll do anything to get my son back. When can I meet him?"

Coopersmith reached into his desk drawer, fished out a business card, and handed it to her. "Just tell him that I referred you to him. He's very busy, so don't be surprised if he tries to put you off for a while."

"Thank you, Mister Coopersmith." She hesitated for a moment. "I noticed you don't have a secretary. If you ever decide to hire one can you keep me in mind?"

"Sure," he said without giving it much thought.

She wrote her name and phone number on a piece of paper and pushed it in front of him. "I really need to find something soon. It would only be temporary until I find a regular job."

"To tell you the truth…Meg." He had to look down at the piece of paper to read her name. "I'm not sure I can afford to pay anyone. And besides, I'm not used to having a secretary. The last one I had was about three years ago. What a pain in the neck.

We were at each other's throats most of the time. It's nothing personal, you understand. I just don't think it would work out."

"I understand," she said, walking toward the door. "Thank you again."

Coopersmith clenched his jaw. "It's only going to be temporary... Why don't you come in tomorrow morning and we'll go over a few things you need to know."

He had done it again. No fee, no client. Nothing to show for his time except a grateful lady who'd talked him into being his secretary.

Eighteen

Eleven o'clock. Meg still hadn't showed up. Maybe she had changed her mind. Or maybe she got sick at the last moment. Whatever the reason, he would give her until noontime. After that she'd be out of luck and out of a job.

The phone rang five minutes later.

"I'm really sorry, Mister Coopersmith," Meg said. "I know you were expecting me and that's why I called. I didn't want you to think that I didn't appreciate what you were trying to do for me. I would've have called sooner, but I had to wait my turn to use the phone."

"Don't tell me you're in jail," Coopersmith said, more disappointed than surprised.

"I was picked up last night off the Boulevard. I don't know why I did it. Maybe I'm not used to people like you being nice to me, or maybe I wanted to get arrested so that I'd have an excuse for not getting Randy back. A social worker told me that one time, and maybe she was right."

"You lied to me, didn't you?"

"Well, I did stop for a while," she said. "But I kept going back to it whenever I needed cash. I didn't tell you because you probably wouldn't have given me the job. Anyway, it doesn't matter anymore, does it?"

She was right. It didn't matter. He wished her luck and said goodbye to her.

He was still thinking about her when the phone rang and

hesitated before answering it. He relaxed a little when he heard Difalco's Brooklyn accent.

"I didn't come up with much. According to the Alabama tracking system, Sarah's mother has an aunt named Jane Carpenter and a cousin, Cassandra Karaman, still living in Mobile. I'll fax everything to you so you can look it over. Maybe I missed something, but it looks like Sarah's mother didn't have much family, at least not in Mobile."

"An aunt and a cousin," Coopersmith repeated. "Well, I guess it'll have to do. By the way, any luck with Sarah's father?"

"I wish I could give you some good news, but I'm afraid it's been too many years since he used the name you gave me. For whatever reason, he dropped the name at the same time he dropped out of sight."

"Well, keep checking. Meanwhile, I'll see what else I can dig up from this end." He paused when he saw Sarah's husband, Mark, walk into the office. "Listen, someone just walked in. I'll talk to you after I get back from Mobile."

Coopersmith remained seated as Mark approached the desk and brusquely said, "I need to speak to you."

"Have a seat," Coopersmith said, motioning toward the chair in front of him.

"I'm not going to be here that long." Mark sounded pissed off, like he wanted to get something off his chest. "I know my wife thinks you're good at what you do, but I'm telling you that ever since she hired you, our life has been in turmoil. That's why I'm here…to see if I can do something about it. All I'm asking is for you to drop the investigation. I'm prepared to pay you a very generous bonus if we can reach an agreement."

Coopersmith looked at Mark for a long moment. "The investigation is not the problem. You know that as well as I do. But even if I backed out, who's to say your wife wouldn't hire somebody else?"

"I know my wife. She trusts only you, and I'll bet my life on it that she'd throw in the towel and go back to being what she used to be."

"What she used to be?"

"Well, you know what I mean. I just want our life to be like before she got so obsessed with finding her birth family."

"She is very determined, I'll grant you that. As for the problems the two of you are having, I really don't want to get involved. It's none of my business."

"Does that mean you're not going to accept my offer?"

"You got it." Coopersmith nodded. "When your wife tells me to stop what I'm doing, I will. But not before."

Mark waited a moment, then turned and walked off in a huff. "Thanks for nothing," he said, just barely loud enough to be heard.

Nineteen

The next day, Coopersmith took the first flight to Mobile and arrived there a little after 1:00 p.m. He had the better of part of the afternoon to check out the names Difalco had given him and to find out what the cops knew of Steve's killer.

His first stop: the Mobile Police Department, where a former Miami FBI clerk named Larry McCaffee was a detective in the homicide unit. He had quit the Bureau twelve years before after being told he wasn't quite good enough to become an agent. Didn't fit the image of what an agent should be, they told him, unofficially.

Coopersmith didn't recognize him at first until he smiled broadly and walked up to shake his hand. Larry now sported a thick moustache and had lost better than twenty pounds. "How the hell are ya?" Larry said, pumping his hand.

"I'm doing okay, and I can see you're doing even better." Coopersmith smiled, happy to see his old friend.

"Let's go into my office and you can tell me what the hell you're doing in my neck of the woods." He led the way through a hallway and into a large office that had part of a wall covered with awards and citations he had received since leaving the Bureau.

"Not bad. Not bad at all." Coopersmith glanced over at the plaque-filled wall.

They sat down to talk and for the first twenty minutes, caught up on old times.

"I'll tell you why I'm here," Coopersmith said. "I'm trying to track down the family of a woman who was adopted." He filled him in on the details and brought him up to date with Difalco's report on Steve Anderson.

"You think the homicide and Sarah's family are connected in some way?" Larry asked.

"I don't know. I hoped you'd help me figure it out."

"Well, I can tell you this—we have zilch to go on. No clues, no witnesses, no suspects, nothing to point us in any direction. The victim was from out of town, which made it even harder to determine a motive. About the only thing we do know is that it probably wasn't a robbery. He had his wallet with forty bucks still in it."

"That's all you have?"

"I'm afraid so. The guy was in town less than twenty-four hours. My hunch is the killer was probably someone he knew."

Coopersmith took a moment to think. "Someone he knew… hmm. Steve has what he thinks is juicy information about Sarah's family and he comes into town and tries to look up some family members."

"And then what?"

"Let's find out. With your brains and my nose and a little luck we might be able to piece this thing together."

They drove out to Jane Carpenter's place not far from town and arrived there ten minutes later.

"Looks abandoned," Coopersmith said as they pulled into the driveway and got out of the car. The house had a couple of broken windows and there were weeds and tall grass growing all over the yard.

"Someone's here," Larry said, pointing to a contented-looking cat with a pink leather collar around its neck. It sat on a rocking chair grooming itself and scarcely took notice of them.

Larry knocked on the door, waited a couple of seconds, and knocked again.

"Who's there?" asked an old woman who sounded like she was just getting over a cold.

"We're with the Mobile Police Department and we need to talk to you," Larry said.

"If it's about my back taxes, you're wasting your time," the old woman said. "I'm broke and I barely have enough money to live on. Why can't you people understand that?"

"We're not here to discuss your back taxes, Missus Carpenter." Larry moved closer to the door. "We want to ask you some questions about a stranger who may have been by to see you a few months ago. His name is Steve Anderson."

"Never heard of him," the woman said after a brief silence.

"Can you please open the door, so I don't have to shout?" Larry said. "It won't take but a few minutes, and we'll be on our way."

The door opened just a bit to allow the old woman, who looked to be at least eighty, to scrutinize the two strangers. After a moment, she opened the door wider. "I don't get too many visitors. What's his name again?"

"Steve Anderson," Larry said. "He came from out of town and could have used a different name."

"He may have dropped by to ask you questions about your family," Coopersmith added.

"What kind of questions?"

Coopersmith hesitated. He was reluctant to reveal too much about the real reason they were there. "Well, he probably tried to find out how much you and your family were worth. You see, the man was a con man with his only objective to figure out a scheme to get some money from you or someone close to you."

"But I don't have any money. You think I'd live like this if I had money? I told him so when he asked if I had a savings account. I told him it was none of his business."

"So he came here," Larry said.

"The name didn't mean anything to me. But when you said he might be a con man, I knew who you were talking about. He didn't stay long, not after he realized I didn't have any money. He mentioned something about having information that would be embarrassing to me, but I didn't pay attention to it. In fact, he stood right where you are when I slammed the door on him."

"Did he ask about your daughter, Cassandra?" Larry asked.

"He did, and I'll tell you the same thing I told him. As far as I'm concerned she's not my daughter any more. She stopped being my daughter the moment she married that Lebanese fella, old enough to be her father. I don't have nothing against people from other cultures, but when she converted to his Muslim religion, well, that was the last straw. I mean, her daddy and I raised her to be a good Christian, and look what she did to us."

Coopersmith and Larry left the old lady's house with a lot of unanswered questions and more than a few theories about Anderson and his ill-fated con game. On the way to Cassandra's office in a building she owned off I-10 near the Mississippi border, they exchanged a few thoughts and agreed that Cassandra probably would turn out to be either a key witness or a prime suspect.

Cassandra Karaman appeared cool and collected as she sat behind her desk and answered questions, mostly from Larry.

"Ever since my husband died, I meet a lot of people, and sometimes complete strangers come in here for one reason or another," she said. "Maybe this man did come in here, but he certainly didn't try to shake me down. Believe me, I would have remembered."

"Your mother said he asked about you," Coopersmith said, trying to get a reaction.

"Look, my mother is very old and she's not all that well up there," she said, pointing to her head. "She gets easily confused, and half the time she doesn't even know what day it is. If you went back to see her again, she'd probably tell you something different."

"That well may be, Missus Karaman," Larry said. "But the fact remains that Steve Anderson was in town for one reason and one reason only. There were two people he wanted to see, and you happen to be one of them."

"Do you have a witness to say he saw us together?"

"Not yet," Larry said. "But we have a lot of leads still to cover." He lifted an eyebrow. "If I were you, I'd think about getting a lawyer."

"A lawyer?" She twisted in her chair. "But why? I haven't done anything. I told you the truth. I never met this Steve Anderson and I had nothing to do with his murder."

Larry and Coopersmith looked at each other, then stood up to leave.

"By the way," Larry said. "Your mother wouldn't happen to be *the* Jane Carpenter, of the Southern Belles of Mobile, would she?"

"Why…yes," Cassandra said. "I'm surprised people still remember her. She co-founded the group and used to be very active until she decided to quit, because of her health, mostly. In case you're wondering, my mother refuses to accept any help from me. I've tried to reach out to her, but she just won't budge, not even if it means saving her house from being taken away from her."

"Well, you know where you can reach me if you change your mind," Larry said, walking away. Coopersmith followed close behind.

"What was that all about?" Coopersmith asked when they were back in the car. "The Southern Belles of Mobile?"

"It's hard to explain, but the Southern Belles of Mobile are like a holdover from the past, when well-bred women took pride in being graceful and charming and, of course, oh so white. Don't get me wrong, they do a lot for the community—blood drives, charity events—but still, I'm going to ask around to see what I can find."

"What will you be looking for?"

"I'm not sure. I've heard a few stories about them—the way they've resisted bringing in minorities into their organization. I don't know what all this has to do with Anderson or his killer—if anything—but I'm going to find out."

"So what do you make of Cassandra?"

"She's holding back on us, that's for sure. The question is how much and why? She didn't impress me as the type who would do the deed herself, but you never know. I think I'm going to give her time to sweat a little, make her think we're getting close to making an arrest."

"How will you do that?"

Larry smiled. "Well, in a few days I'll *accidentally* leak something to the press. You know, the usual bullshit thing. Some off-the-record statement that we have a good suspect and that an arrest is imminent. Meanwhile, we'll keep an eye on her, where she goes, who she meets. If my hunch is right, we're going to find she's not in this thing alone."

When they got back to town, Larry dropped Coopersmith off at his hotel. They made plans to get together later in the evening for drinks and some more reminiscing about their days with the Bureau.

"I'll bring a fax I got from Difalco the other day," Larry said, before driving off. "That guy has more stories, half of which I think he made up just to keep us in stitches. See you later."

The next morning, Coopersmith caught the first flight back to Miami. He had left the case in good hands. Nothing more to do but wait for Larry to get back to him.

Twenty

Coopersmith called Sarah later in the day and gave her a rundown on his trip to Mobile. He was still on the phone with her when he heard a fax coming in. "Hold on. I'm getting a fax from Difalco. Let me read it to you."

"There had been a state bulletin about a homeless man known by the nickname 'the Preacher,' who had recently been found wandering the streets of downtown Miami. He appeared disoriented and confused and had no identification on him except an old library card with the name Amos Matthews. Police had detained him and placed him in a holding ward at Jackson Memorial Hospital, where they expected him to remain for the next couple of days. The man was described as being in his mid-sixties, medium dark complexion, five feet ten inches tall, one hundred sixty pounds, gray hair."

"My God, if he's my father, I want to know. When can you check it out?"

"First thing tomorrow morning."

"Call me the moment you know something…anything."

"Don't get your hopes up just yet. It could turn out to be anyone."

"You're right," she said, her voice dropping. "It's too early to jump to any conclusions."

"Good, then I'll talk to you tomorrow."

"Oh, before I forget, Mark came to see me the day before yesterday. We had a long talk. He wants me to come back. He says he's willing to put everything behind us if I will simply drop what I'm doing. I'm telling you this because I have a feeling he may want to talk to you about it."

"I wouldn't have mentioned it, but he was already here."

"What did you tell him?"

"Not a whole lot. Basically that you were the boss and I'd stay on the case until you told me otherwise."

"He's really not a bad person, you know. Before all this came up about my natural family, he was the kindest, sweetest man a woman could want. We had a very good marriage up until…I don't know why I'm telling you this. It has nothing to do with the reason I hired you, does it?"

"No, it doesn't. But since you brought it up, I think you should ask yourself whether or not you still want to continue the investigation, especially if the lead tomorrow turns out to be another dead end. You said yourself, you had a good marriage before this whole thing started."

"I appreciate what you're trying to do, but the question you raised got answered the day I got Morrison's first phone call. I may love my husband, but I'm not about to back away from the truth just because he can't or won't accept that I happen to be part black."

"Like I told your husband, you're a very determined lady, and you've proven it once again. I'll call you tomorrow, no matter what it turns out to be."

After she hung up the phone, Sarah told Dolores about the news from Difalco and the possibility that the homeless man might be her father.

"That's great," Dolores said. "But you seem a little down. What else did Coopersmith say?"

"Nothing…nothing I hadn't thought about before. He said I should consider whether continuing the investigation is still something I want to do, especially now that Mark wants to patch things up and put everything behind us."

"Well, I'm the last one to know about what makes a good

marriage, considering I've struck out twice. But, if you want my opinion…"

The phone rang and Dolores got up to answer it. "It's for you," She cupped her hand over the mouthpiece. "It's Mark. We'll continue our conversation later and I'll tell you *exactly* what I think you should do." She smiled and handed her the phone and left to go into another room.

"I'm not sure he's the person I'm looking for," Coopersmith said standing in front of the nurses' station at Jackson Memorial hospital. "But I'll know after I ask him a few questions."

"Amos Matthews. Yes, I think he's the homeless man brought in here the day before yesterday," the nurse said. "Didn't give us a name, so we used the one on an old library card he had on him." She checked a list of patients admitted within the past few days and found his name with a line drawn across it. "We released him early this morning."

"You mean he's gone? But he was obviously mentally disturbed. The bulletin said he was confused and disoriented. How could he have been released?"

"We issue those bulletins on a regular basis. You know how many homeless people are brought in each week for one reason or another? More than half have mental problems. It's just a phrase we use to describe them, that's all. The fact is, we're terribly overcrowded and we're not a social service agency. That's why we release them within twenty-four to forty-eight hours if we don't get a call from a relative or a close friend."

Coopersmith felt his face grow hot. "Well, where did you release him to or did you just kick him out the door?"

"Look, you don't have to get sarcastic." She glared at him. "We do the best we can. The police picked him up and dropped him off at Saint Jude's, a place for the homeless on Second Avenue."

"Thanks." He rushed off.

St. Jude's was nearby, on the other side of I-95.

Several men milled around. None looked like the man described in the bulletin. Inside the shelter, more men, of all ages and races. They were seated at long tables eating sandwiches and slurping hot soup from white plastic bowls like the kind they use in hospitals. He walked up and down between the tables, and paused when he saw a bearded, middle-aged man coming toward him.

"You seem to be looking for someone," said the man. "I'm Brother James."

"His name is Amos Matthews," Coopersmith said. "He got dropped off here early this morning."

"The name doesn't mean anything to me. What does he look like?"

"He's in his mid-sixties, gray hair, and he's black, with a medium dark complexion."

"That describes several men who come in here on a regular basis. You're welcome to drop by later this evening. We get a different crowd for dinner. He may be among them."

"Thanks. I might just do that. By the way, his street name is the Preacher, if that means anything."

Brother James nodded. "The Preacher. Yes, I know who you're talking about. I don't know his birth name, but he comes in here every once in a while. Sometimes I won't see him for weeks and then he suddenly appears. Likes to keep to himself, which is not that unusual with a lot of the men who come here."

"Why do they call him the Preacher?"

"Well, he used to stand on street corners quoting scriptures and talking about the end of the world. He's a little strange but he's basically harmless, which is why the police usually leave him alone. May I ask why you're looking for him?"

"Just trying to help someone out," Coopersmith said, handing across his business card. He asked Brother James to call the next time the Preacher came in for a meal.

After giving Sarah an update, Coopersmith spent the next

two hours driving from one homeless haunt to another. Twice he thought he spotted him, but each time it turned out to be somebody else.

Coopersmith was heading back to his office when he got the first beep, followed by a second with a 911 at the end. He pulled over to the nearest phone.

"Just got a call from Cassandra's lawyer," Larry said. "She's ready to sit down and talk. If you just happened to be in town and just happened to be in my office, tomorrow morning, say around nine, well…I guess you'd just have to sit in on the interview."

"Say no more. I'm on the next plane to Mobile. I owe you one, ole buddy."

TWENTY-ONE

"Before we start," said Cassandra's attorney, seated next to her across from Larry's desk, "we want to make it very clear that my client had nothing whatsoever to do with the murder of Steve Anderson. However, she does know certain facts about a possible suspect, and that's why we're here. She's prepared to cooperate fully and answer all questions having to do with this matter."

"Why don't we start from the beginning?" Larry said. "Tell us what you know about this so-called suspect." He leaned forward and scribbled the date and Cassandra's name at the top of a steno pad. Coopersmith did the same on a small note pad that he pulled from the pocket of his coat.

"It started with this man, Steve Anderson, who as you know visited my mother," Cassandra said. "He also paid me a visit at my office and he told me this incredible story about my cousin, Rebecca, whom I lost track of many years ago. Her children were half black, he said, and he threatened to spread the story around town. He'd done his homework and he knew about my mother being one of the founders of the Southern Belles of Mobile, which I have to admit has a history of being very racist, though they deny it publicly. Anyway, he demanded ten thousand dollars to keep the information about Rebecca's children from being made public."

"I think I know where you're heading with this," Larry said.

"Well, if you do, you'll know I did it for her. I paid the money so my mother would be spared the humiliation of being ostracized by the Southern Belles because of something over which she had no control. And don't think for a moment those old biddies wouldn't have done it. They've expelled people for far less."

Larry took quick notes as he listened. "You mentioned a possible suspect. What's his name? What does he look like?"

"His name is Jerry…Jerry Bradley. He's in his mid-thirties, green eyes, longish blond hair, and a dark birth mark above his left eye. He's the one that actually delivered the money to Steve. Being a woman alone, I've found it necessary to rely on people like Jerry to help me out now and then. At over two hundred pounds and close to six feet tall, he can be pretty intimidating. I figured that if Jerry delivered the money, Steve would get the message that he'd have to tangle with him if he ever came back and bothered me again."

"Did you talk to Jerry after that, to make sure he had delivered the money?" Coopersmith asked.

"Of course. He called and said everything had gone well. But we never talked about Steve again. It was like it never happened, which was fine with me. I tried calling him at his home a few days later, but his phone had been disconnected." She paused to retrieve a piece of paper with Jerry's address and phone number on it and handed it to Larry.

"Why didn't you tell us this the day we went to your office?" Larry asked.

"I feared you would think I had something to do with it…considering I paid him to keep his mouth shut. I know I should've told you the truth, but…"

"How do we know you're telling us the truth now?" Larry asked.

Her attorney interrupted. "I think we answered that question at the beginning, Lieutenant McCaffee. My client has no reason to lie, certainly not at this point. She came here of her own volition to provide information about Jerry Bradley, and to answer your questions, which I think she has done very well. Other than lie when you first questioned her, she did nothing wrong. She was a victim of a blackmailer, pure and simple, and she used poor judgment in the way she handled the situation. We can discuss her judgment if you like, but that isn't going to accomplish anything, is it?"

"How well did you know Jerry?" Coopersmith asked.

"I've known him ever since he was a little boy. I was a friend of his mother, who died when he was in his teens. He's basically been on his own ever since. I kind of felt sorry for him, so I helped him out as much as I could. But if he had something to do with Steve's murder, well, friend or no friend, that's where I draw the line."

"I want you to do something for me." Larry put down his pen. "Over the next few days, I want you to write down the names of everyone who knew or had anything to do with Jerry. His friends, business associates, girls he ran around with, anyone who might be able to tell us something about him and where we might find him. We'll talk again in a few days…that is, if you're still willing to cooperate." He stood up to indicate the interview had ended. Cassandra and her attorney got up and prepared to leave.

"We were hoping today's interview would be the end of it," the attorney said. "But if you feel it necessary to speak to my client again, then of course, she'd be willing to answer further questions. All I ask is that you call me first so I can make the proper arrangements if it's going to be another session like we had today."

After Cassandra and her attorney left, Larry and Coopersmith compared notes. They agreed that Cassandra held something back, maybe not a lot, but enough to make them wonder how much she really knew about Steve's murder.

"You know what I think," Larry said, looking over his notes which he scribbled too quickly for anyone but himself to make out. "I think she hired Jerry to do more than just deliver the money. I think she wanted Jerry to teach him a lesson, maybe rough him up a bit. But it went too far and he killed him."

"Well, at least we have a name," Coopersmith said. "I have a feeling Jerry has left Mobile for good, which means an arrest won't be easy, assuming he's the one who did it."

"That's why I'm depending on you," Larry said, pointing at him. "You know more about his movements than anyone, and sooner or later you're going to come across him. I just know you are. And when you do, I want to be the first person you call. Deal?"

"You got it." Coopersmith grinned. "I said I owed you one and I meant it."

"I just thought of something," Larry said. "You think Brewster could help us out?"

"What did you have in mind?"

Larry shrugged. "Well, if Jerry should contact him, it sure would be nice to know where and when he plans to make a payoff. Since you already know him, you could give him a call and lay it out for him. Maybe pump up the killer angle. He's killed once, he may do it again. That kind of thing."

Coopersmith shook his head. "I don't know. When I talked to him, he was pretty skittish. Wouldn't even admit the blackmailer already put the squeeze on him. It's worth a try, I guess. But don't be surprised if he tells me to take a hike." He looked at his watch. "If I leave now, I just might make an early flight to Miami. We can kick some ideas around on the way to the airport."

Back in Miami, Coopersmith called Sarah and talked to her for almost half an hour. She was full of questions, for which he had few answers, except for the big one—the blackmailer's identity.

"I want you to know that I've given it a lot of thought...about whether or not I should continue with this. I talked it over with Dolores and I have to admit she's right. What's happening is too important to put aside just because I'm having problems with my husband. She made me see that even if I dropped the investigation, there is no guarantee my relationship with Mark will be any better. So to answer your question from yesterday, I want to see it through to the end."

"I'm glad to hear that. Personally, I think…never mind, it's really none of my business." He thought Mark was a jerk for letting Sarah's father come between them. "I might check out a few more homeless hangouts. I'll call you if I find anything."

A few minutes later, Coopersmith picked up the phone and dialed Brewster's number, but there was no answer. He tried calling the station where he worked and got put on hold. Seconds later, Brewster came on the line.

"Hello."

"This is Joe Coopersmith from Miami. Before you hang up on me, this has nothing to do with Sarah or the reason I went to your house. Just hear me out and I'll tell you why I'm calling."

"I'm listening, but make it fast, I've got to be on the air in a couple of minutes."

"It's a long story, but I'm working with the Mobile Police Department on a homicide. Turns out the guy who tried to blackmail you got the information from the man he killed. That's right—the guy is a cold-blooded murderer. He's killed once and could do it again. If I were you, I'd be real careful if and when he should happen to call you. You just never know what might trigger him off like it did in Mobile."

"What's…his name?"

"Jerry Bradley. The Mobile Police Department has already issued a state-wide bulletin on him. All they want to do is locate him and put him in prison where he belongs. Obviously you can help us by giving me a call the next time you hear from him. That's basically it in a nutshell."

There was a long silence. "Without admitting to anything, I really hope you get him."

"Does that mean you'll give me a call?"

"Sure. If and when he should call me, I'll let you know."

"Thanks," Coopersmith said.

Afterwards, he thought that Brewster had been too polite, too quick to say yes, all of which meant that it would be a snowy day in July before he'd hear from him.

Brewster waited until the next commercial break before dialing the Fixer's number. He answered after the third ring.

"It's me, Brewster. I'm calling just like you told me. That private investigator from Miami called a few minutes ago and said the blackmailer—Jerry Bradley, he said his name was—is wanted for killing a guy in Mobile. He asked me to help him…to call the next time I heard from Bradley."

"You admitted you were being blackmailed?"

"No, I really didn't tell him anything. I just listened and told him that if I heard from this guy, I would call."

"Good. As long as you keep to your story that you've never had anything to do with him, there's nothing they can do about it."

"One more thing. He said the Mobile Police Department issued a state bulletin on Bradley."

"That means there's probably a picture of him and a good description. Great. Just keep doing what you're doing and call me the minute you hear something."

Twenty-Two

She looked to be in her thirties—considered over the hill for a nude dancer. In a business where young, firm tits were everything, she had maybe two, three years left at the most. Already, the manager had begun to soften the lights above her so the customers would not see the telltale wrinkles around her eyes and the natural sagging under her breasts.

From a table in the back of the dark, smoke-filled room, a man who'd had too many drinks watched as Stella stroked her crotch with one hand and her full, round breasts with the other. "Why don't you come over and sit on my face?" he yelled.

Stella was used to guys saying things like that and she really didn't mind. It made it easy for her to decide who her pigeon would be, for later after she had finished her set. From experience, she'd learned that an already drunk, loudmouthed jerk was a perfect mark for the old overpriced bottle of champagne routine for which she stood to make a nice commission.

When she finished dancing, she went backstage and a few minutes later came out wearing a black, see-through outfit. She made a beeline to where the guy with the big mouth was sitting.

"Hi, my name's Stella," she said with a put-on smile. "Want some company?"

"Sure, why not," he said. "Can I buy you a drink?"

"How about some champagne? I really love champagne."

"Champagne for the lady," he shouted to the waitress. "And another whiskey sour for me."

"You from Miami?"

"I'm from Mobile," he answered, stretching out the first syllable.

"I've never been there, but I used to have a friend who came from there. She used to dance here, but she left to get married and start a family, if you can believe that. Families are nice, I guess. What about you? Do you have family?"

"Fuck families. Who needs them, anyway? I never even knew my mother. The bitch got knocked up and didn't know what to do with me, so she gave me away right after I was born. And you know what? She had more kids, four of them. Can you believe that?"

The waitress interrupted, placing his drink in front of him and the bottle of champagne and a glass in the middle of the table. "That'll be a hundred dollars," she said without batting an eyelash.

The man pulled out a wad of money, plucked out a couple of fifties, and handed them to her.

"Like I said, families suck," he said after the waitress left. He paused to pour some champagne into her glass. "But you know what? It doesn't matter, because I'm better than all my brothers and sisters put together. And you want to know why?" He took a quick gulp of his drink. "I know something about them, something they'd just as soon people not know, if you get what I mean." He suddenly stood up and excused himself to go the men's room.

After he had relieved himself, he stepped up to a phone near a condom-dispensing machine and dialed a number he knew from memory. "Just thought I'd call to see how you were doing," he said, slurring his words.

"You're drunk," Brewster said. "Can't you pick on somebody else for a change?"

"Very funny, but not funny enough. The reason…"

The manager's voice suddenly came through an overhead speaker. "The Body Double would like to introduce a new dancer who just arrived from New Orleans," he shouted. "Her name is Sherri L'Amour. Why don't you give her a big hand and make her feel welcome." Loud whistling could be heard in the background.

"Like I started to say, the reason I called was because I heard something. I heard you finally made the big time, which means we're going to have to change our arrangement. You make more bucks, so I make more bucks. That's only fair, don't you think?"

"I don't know what you heard, but it's just in the talking stage, nothing firm. I'm not even sure I want to take it."

"Cut the crap. The guy who told me works right there at your station. I'm sure I don't have to remind you what a well-placed phone call will do to your Big Apple job that you claim is just in the talking stage."

"Okay, okay, I get the message. Just back off a little, all right? Maybe we can reach an understanding."

"I knew you'd see it my way. Now listen. As soon as you get to New York, I want to see a weekly donation coming my way. It doesn't have to be big in the beginning, but it does have to be on time. We'll work out the details later. Oh, before I forget…congratulations." He chuckled as he hung up the phone.

Brewster pressed the disconnect button, then dialed the Fixer's number. "It's me, Brewster. I just spoke to him. He called to let me know that he knew about my job in New York."

"What else did he say?"

"He wants more money, of course, but not until I get to New York."

"Now think for a moment. Is there anything he said that might indicate where he was calling from?"

"He was drunk, if that means anything, and he must have called from some bar, maybe a nightclub."

"What makes you say that?"

"I could hear an overhead speaker in the background. Something about a dancer named Sherri, Sherri from New Orleans, I think he said. And the name of the place was called Body...Body something. I can't remember."

"That's good, Mister Brewster. I have a feeling everything's going to turn out just fine. Call me if you hear from him again."

The man sat back at his table, smiling broadly.

"I think I'm getting to like this town. Maybe I'll stick around a few more days." He slipped his hand beneath the table and dropped it, onto her lap.

"It's okay. You can feel me if you want." Then she added, "When you order champagne, it's included."

"Well, actually, that's not all I had in mind." He slipped his fingers deep into her crotch. "Maybe later when you get off..."

"Sorry." She shook her head, "but I don't do windows and I don't fuck for money."

The man shrugged and signaled the waitress to bring him another drink. "You can't blame a guy for trying." His smile faded.

Twenty-Three

"You wanted me to call you when the Preacher came in," Brother James said. "He's sitting at one of the tables. Better hurry if you want to see him."

"Thanks, I'm on my way," Coopersmith said, quickly hanging up.

When Coopersmith arrived at the shelter twenty minutes later, the Preacher had left.

"You just missed him," Brother James said, walking toward him. "One minute he was eating a sandwich and the next he was out the door."

Coopersmith noticed a group of visitors at the other end of the room. One of them had a camera and he was snapping pictures.

"Did he take any pictures when the Preacher was here?" he asked.

"Why, yes. Come to think of it, that's when the Preacher got up and left."

"Can you do me a favor? Can you get copies and let me know if you spot the guy?"

"I'll be glad to."

Coopersmith reached for his wallet, pulled out a fifty-dollar bill, and handed it to Brother James. "For the shelter," he said. "Keep up the good work."

Coopersmith unlocked his office door as the phone rang.

He rushed to answer it. Larry called with some interesting news about Cassandra.

"I just hung up from speaking with her," Larry said. "She admitted she hadn't been entirely truthful. Turns out she actually told Jerry to give Steve a good beating, to teach him a lesson. Just like we figured. She knew Steve was dead because afterwards, Jerry called and told her he'd gone a little too far, that he didn't mean to kill him."

"Did she see him after that?"

"She claims not. She said she just hung up on him and never had anything more to do with him after that."

"So what next?"

"She's coming in with her lawyer to provide a formal statement, and after that it's up to the prosecutor to decide what he wants to do. My guess is, he'll probably want to cut a deal and use her as a witness against Jerry." He paused for a second. "There's something else she told me…not about the murder but about Sarah's mother. You're not going to believe this, but Jerry is actually her second cousin. Her cousin Rebecca was seventeen when she got pregnant with Jerry, and she gave him up for adoption shortly after his birth."

There was a short pause. "Listen, do you mind if I give Cassandra a call, just to talk about Sarah's mother? Maybe now might be the right time to tell her about Sarah and the reason she hired me."

"No problem, go ahead. Just let me know if she tells you something about the case."

"Thanks." Coopersmith hung up, then dialed Cassandra's number from a card he'd picked up at her office. She answered on the second ring and put him on hold.

"I'm sorry, but I had someone on the other line," she said a moment later. "If you're calling about my case, I already spoke to Lieutenant McCaffee."

"Actually, I called about what you said to him…about Rebecca."

"What about her?"

"I didn't want to tell you before, but the truth is her daughter Sarah, hired me to track down her natural family. She, her sister and two brothers, were all given up for adoption. You should also know that Jerry has used the information he got from Steve to blackmail his half-brothers and sisters, including Sarah."

Cassandra sighed. "In a way, I'm not surprised. He was very bitter toward his mother for giving him up the way she did. And he was also a bit of an opportunist, which explains why he decided to continue with Steve's blackmail scheme."

"This is probably not the right time to ask, but do you think you might want to talk to Sarah?"

"I think I would," she said after a brief silence. "Sarah should know that her mother was a sweet, wonderful girl. Too trusting, perhaps, but basically a warm-hearted person who had a way of making friends with almost everyone she met."

"Great. I'll let Sarah know how you feel. About the case… Larry McCaffee is a fair man. Just play straight with him from now on and things will work out. Good luck."

After he had hung up, Coopersmith called Sarah and received a busy signal. He tried again a minute later and she answered almost immediately.

"Are you sitting down?" he asked.

"I am now. What is it?"

"I got a call from Larry McCaffee and he told me something that's almost hard to believe, but it's true. Jerry, the guy who tried to blackmail you, well, turns out he's your half-brother. Before coming to Florida, your mother gave him up for adoption." Coopersmith repeated everything Larry and Cassandra had told him, and when he finished, he said, "I hope you don't mind that I told her about you."

"I don't understand. If he's my brother, why is he doing this?"

"Cassandra would be a better person to answer that. She said she'd like to talk to you. She sounded like she really meant it." He gave Sarah Cassandra's number. "It'd be best not to discuss the case with her," he added. "You wouldn't want to wind up having to testify against her."

Twenty-Four

When the operator asked if he would accept the call, Coopersmith agreed.

"It's good to hear from you, Daniel. How's it going?"

"The board approved my parole," Daniel said with restrained excitement. "I should be out in three or four weeks. I don't know what I would've done if they'd turned me down."

"Congratulations. Have you thought any more about Sarah…whether you'd like to meet her?"

Daniel hesitated. "What would be the point? We come from different worlds and nothing can change that. The person I *do* want to meet is my father. That's why I'm calling. I hoped you might've found him by now."

"As a matter of fact, I'm working on some information about someone who may or may not be your father. He's a homeless person, which means he could be almost anywhere."

"Do you think you'll find him by the time I get to Miami? It would mean a lot to me if I could meet him. That is, if he turns out to be my father."

"With some luck, I may find him this week or the next. Then again, it may take longer. It's hard to say."

"Well, just keep me in mind. If we don't talk before I get released, I'll see you in Miami."

"I'll be looking for you," Coopersmith said.

Two days later, Coopersmith got the call he'd been expecting. Brother James had a photograph of the Preacher. "So this is him." Coopersmith sat at a table across from Brother James. He held the photograph in his hand and studied it closely. The man had a thin, semi-angular face, gray hair and a medium-dark complexion. "You know what? He looks a lot like his son Daniel. It's him, all right. Now all I have to do is find him."

"I've asked a few of the men if they'd seen him, and one said he had been spending a lot of time by the river under the Flagler Street bridge."

"Do you mind if I keep this?"

Brother James nodded. "You can have it. I'm sure you'll find him sooner or later and when you do, well, I hope everything turns out all right. Don't be surprised if he gives you a hard time. Homeless men tend to be a little suspicious of people they don't know. If I were you, I would ease into the reason you want to talk to him."

"Thanks for the tip." Coopersmith slipped the photograph into his coat pocket. "I really appreciate your help. If there's anything I can do for you or the shelter, you know where to reach me."

Brother James thought about it for a second. "As a matter of fact, there is something you can do for me. You heard about the homeless woman whose body was found a couple of days ago?"

"By the old cemetery? The paper said she died of a heart attack and she had no family."

"Well, she may have been homeless, but she *did* have a family. She had a daughter who's fairly well off, I've been told. They hadn't seen each other in years. Apparently they weren't that close and for whatever reason, the daughter wants nothing to do with her mother's body. That means the poor woman will be buried in a pauper's grave, which as you know is a terrible way to end up."

Coopersmith nodded slowly, tapping his temple with his finger. "You want me to talk to the daughter, is that what you're asking?"

Brother James smiled. "Exactly. I tried calling, but she was very curt…said she had no interest in discussing her mother's funeral plans."

"What makes you think she'll listen to me?"

Brother James shrugged. "She may not, but with you being a professional investigator, well, I just thought you might have better luck."

"Do you have her address?"

"I'll get it for you." Brother James stepped into his office and returned with a sheet of paper. "All the information you'll need is on this sheet."

Coopersmith took the paper and gave it a quick glance over. The daughter's address was a condo in a luxury building on Key Biscayne.

"I'll give it a try. But don't be surprised if I come back empty-handed."

"I have faith in you," Brother James said with a smile. "Just do your best."

"Give me a couple of days," Coopersmith walked off. Just outside the shelter a homeless man ran up to him. The man smelled as though he hadn't bathed in a month and he had a desperate look on his face.

"I heard you were looking for the Preacher," he said, his voice husky. "I know where he hangs out."

"Where?"

"What's it worth to you? I just need a couple of bucks or whatever you can spare. But don't tell Brother James."

Coopersmith reached for his wallet and pulled out a five-dollar bill and handed it him. "Okay, where does he hang out?"

"There's a little park near Thirty-Sixth Street, next to the causeway to Miami Beach. He spends a lot of time there when he's not out walking the streets. He's a little strange, you know. Talks to himself a lot...doesn't make sense half the time."

"Thanks," Coopersmith said. The man crossed the street to join a friend and head down the street, probably in search of a liquor store.

Coopersmith knew the area well, and parked his car along

the side of the street. He sat there for a couple of minutes, then got out and walked into the park. "Nice day, isn't it?" he said as he strolled up to an elderly couple sitting on a bench.

"Lovely," answered the woman. "Not a cloud in the sky."

"Come here often?"

"Every day," the man said. "When you get to be our age, it's the little pleasures in life that mean a lot. Don't miss the north for nothing."

"I'm looking for someone, a homeless man who spends a lot of time here," Coopersmith said. "His daughter hired me to find him." He pulled out the photograph of the Preacher and showed it to them. "Does he look familiar?"

The man shook his head. "No, can't say I've seen him before."

"He looks a little familiar, but to be honest I never paid attention," said the woman. "They don't come around here anymore—the homeless, that is. The police came in a few days ago and ordered them out of the park. They never bothered us, but I guess a few people must've complained."

"Thanks just the same." Coopersmith said.

Coopersmith left the park and drove to Key Biscayne, a small island community near downtown Miami where an odd mix of residents—winter tourists, nouveau riche, and semi-retired drug smugglers—made for an interesting place to visit. When he got to the building where the dead woman's daughter lived, he slowed down at a guard house.

"I'd like to see the manager," Coopersmith said as he pulled up to the window.

"Is she expecting you?" asked the young man with a heavy Haitian accent.

"No, but someone told me she could help me find a condo."

The guard took a moment to jot down the car's plate number. "Go ahead. The office is around the corner next to the pool area. Just park in any visitor's slot." He raised the gate to allow Coopersmith to enter the compound.

Out of sight from the guardhouse, Coopersmith pulled into the nearest empty slot, parked, and walked into the building. He took the elevator to a 9th-floor condo, a corner unit overlooking the ocean, and rang the bell.

A few seconds later, a woman opened the door. About forty, with a roundish, pretty face and a thin, graceful build that made her look taller than she really was. She wore a soft yellow sundress that came down to the top of her slippers.

"Elizabeth Conners?"

She nodded. "Yes, can I help you?"

"My name is Joe Coopersmith and I'd like to talk to you about…about your mother."

"Are you with the police?"

"No, I'm a private investigator. If I can just have a moment of your time…"

"I'm sorry, but I have nothing to say to you." She started to close the door.

"She loved you very much."

After a long pause, she closed her eyes and sighed. "Come in," she said, her voice somber. She led the way to the couch in the living room. "Please have a seat. What do you know about my mother?"

"The truth?" Coopersmith sat down. "Not very much."

"Then you lied." She sat down on the couch a safe distance away from him.

"I'm sorry, but I had to talk to you and I wanted to get your attention. Look, I'm here because Brother James asked me to come. He's very concerned that your mother is going to be buried in a pauper's grave. I'm sure you have your reasons for not wanting to assume responsibility, but…"

"I do have my reasons, Mister Coopersmith, and frankly they are none of your business. I'm sure Brother James means well and so do you, but my decision is final. It's a family matter and I'd like to keep it that way."

Coopersmith hesitated. "When I told you your mother loved

you very much, it meant something to you, didn't it?"

Elizabeth lips quivered. "I was…surprised, that's all. My mother and I never got along and when she had her stroke a few years ago I was expected to care for her. I'm an only child and people *expected* me to take care of her. But they didn't know… how could they?"

"I think I'm beginning to understand," Coopersmith said.

"Well, then maybe you should know the whole story. Maybe it's better if someone knows that I'm not the selfish, insensitive daughter who doesn't want to provide for her mother's burial."

"I didn't come here to make you feel uncomfortable or even guilty about it. You really don't owe me or anyone else an explanation."

She attempted a smile. "Thank you for saying that. But like I said, someone should know that I'm not entirely heartless. Stubborn, maybe, but not heartless." She paused. "Would you like a cup of coffee or a cold drink?"

"Anything diet would be fine."

She got up and went to the kitchen, and returned a moment later carrying a tray with two glasses, a can of diet cola, and a bottle of Perrier. "It won't be easy to talk about this, especially with a stranger," she said, pouring the drinks into the glasses. She placed them on the coffee table and sat back down on the couch.

"When I was a young girl," she continued, "my father died and my mother eventually remarried. In the beginning everything was great. I felt lucky to have such a wonderful stepfather. He was kind and very generous. Then when he lost his job, he started spending a lot of time at home. That's when it started."

"The abuse?"

"No, the long talks. We would talk for hours sometimes, about everything. He knew so much about so many things. He had traveled all over the world and met all kinds of interesting people. I was just a young girl and so in awe of him, so much so that I didn't realize what was happening. When he first touched me, something inside me knew it was wrong, but I was confused.

Here was this man who had been so kind and loving, and all of a sudden he wanted to make me do things I didn't want to do."

"Did you tell your mother?"

She shook her head. "Not in the beginning. I was afraid. Afraid she'd blame me." She took a sip of water. "When I finally did tell her, she didn't believe me. Not until I was fifteen years old did she realize that something was wrong." Her voice cracked. "By then I was four months pregnant. Even then she didn't believe me. My stepfather convinced her it must've been one of my boyfriends, which was crazy because I didn't know that many boys and my mother knew that."

"Look, you don't have to…"

"I want to finish," she said, regaining her composure. "It was my stepfather's idea. He said he knew of this doctor who could make it *go away*, as he put it…like nothing had ever happened. He took me to this so-called doctor's home somewhere in South Miami. I'll never forget it. It was like a nightmare. He couldn't stop the bleeding and the next thing I remember is waking up in the emergency room at Jackson Memorial Hospital." She looked out the window for a long moment. "To save my life, the doctors had to perform a hysterectomy," she said quietly.

"That's quite a story," Coopersmith said with a sigh. "What about your mother? Did she still refuse to believe you?"

"She didn't want to talk about it. Even after my stepfather left her for another woman. She *still* refused to believe that he had sexually abused me for so many years. Later, after I had left the house for good, we hardly spoke to one another. I went on with my life, got married to a man from Dallas, got divorced, and eventually lost track of her. I didn't know she had died until I got the phone call from Brother James. To be honest, I felt absolutely nothing when he told me." She slowly got up and walked over to an antique hutch. She picked up a doll and held it for a moment.

"I've had this doll since I was seven. My father gave it to me for my birthday. You may not understand because you're a man, but every little girl's fantasy is that she will someday be a mother.

Thanks to my mother and stepfather, I will never have the pleasure of ever becoming one."

Coopersmith sat silently for a couple of seconds, then got up. "I'm sorry. I'll try my best to explain to Brother James."

"I'll make a deal with you, Mister Coopersmith. I'll do whatever Brother James thinks is best…on one condition."

"What's that?"

"That you find my stepfather. I'll pay you for your services, of course."

"That's it?"

"That's it."

"You got a deal," he said with a smile.

She stepped across the room to a small desk and retrieved an old letter addressed to her mother. "There's his name and his last known address," she said, handing him the envelope.

"It's none of my business, but why do you want to find him?"

"Now that my mother is dead, I suddenly have this need to know what happened to him." She shook her head in confusion. "I'm not sure I can explain it. Maybe it's because he's the only one who knows the truth. Not that it matters anymore." She looked at Coopersmith. "Does that make any sense?"

He nodded. "Knowing everything you've told me, I think it does. I'll call you the moment I know something."

TWENTY-FIVE

Cassandra immediately recognized the voice. "I told you never to call me again. The police know all about you."

"You sold me out, didn't you?" Jerry said. "And in case you forgot, I did it for you. I'm sure the cops would love to hear my side of the story."

"First of all, I didn't go to the police. They came to me after a private investigator from Miami tied me to Steve's blackmail scheme. And secondly, I never told you to kill him. Did I?"

"It was an accident," Jerry said defensively. "He struggled and I had to whack him a few times. If you hadn't sent me there in the first place, the guy would be alive today and I wouldn't be on the run. Think about *that*, dear cousin."

"Well, I didn't tell you to rob him."

"What are you talking about?"

"I know all about it…what you did with the information in the briefcase. How could you stoop so low?"

"Who told you? The private eye? Well, what did you expect me to do? I was broke and you certainly didn't offer to help. Which brings me to the point of this call."

"Forget it. I'm not giving you any money, not after what you did to your half brothers and sisters."

"Fuck my brothers and sisters and fuck you. You owe me and I aim to collect. Just consider it a debt for services rendered. I'll call you in a few days…or I might just surprise you and pay you a personal visit." He chuckled and hung up.

Cassandra removed the small microphone from the handset, hung up, then pressed the off button on the recorder that Lieutenant McCaffee had given her. She tried calling him at his office, but he had left for the day.

"Just tell him to call me," she said to the woman who answered. "Better yet, if he can drop by my office sometime tomorrow, I've got something for him to pick up."

It didn't take long for Difalco to research the name Coopersmith had given him. It was a Polish name, not too common, which, combined with his approximate age, made it easy to trace. Standing next to his desk, Coopersmith read Difalco's fax.

Joe,
You said you just wanted a locate so here it is: Frank J. Cimoszewicz died of natural causes on December 2, 1992 in Chicago. At the time he lived with his wife, Thelma and her two children from a previous marriage. If you want a full report, let me know and I'll send it on down to you.

The fax still in his hand, Coopersmith sat down and dialed Elizabeth's number. "It's Joe Coopersmith," he said the moment he heard her answer. "I got the information you wanted."

"You found him?" she asked, sounding a little surprised.

"Yeah, with the help of a buddy who checked every data bank in the country. Your stepfather died of natural causes in nineteen ninety-two in Chicago. He had a wife and two stepchildren."

After a brief silence, Elizabeth said, "I don't know why, but I feel a little sad…not for him, but for my mother. She really did love him, you know. And during the time they were together, I think he loved her."

"If you want a full report…"

"It won't be necessary," she said, her voice fading to almost a whisper. "You've been very understanding and I really appreciate it. Thank you. Thank you for everything."

Coopersmith was still at his desk when the phone rang.

"Hope you're calling about the Preacher," Coopersmith said to Brother James, leaning back in his chair. "I sure could use a good tip right about now."

"Actually, I called about Elizabeth's mother. You did so much to make it happen, I thought you would want to know that the funeral will be tomorrow at ten in the morning at Southern Memorial Park on West Dixie Highway. Nothing fancy, just a priest and maybe a few of the homeless who knew her."

"Ten o'clock…I don't know if I can make it, but thanks for letting me know."

"I understand. If you change your mind, well, you know where we'll be."

For the rest of the day, Coopersmith checked every homeless hangout he could think of within a three-mile radius of downtown Miami. He had the Preacher's photo and glanced at it every time he saw a black man fitting the Preacher's general description. Having the photo helped, but it wasn't enough. There were just too many places where a homeless man could be, assuming he were still around, that he hadn't moved north to Hollywood, Dania, or Fort Lauderdale or any of the endless list of coastal towns.

Coopersmith stopped at a light on Biscayne Boulevard at 33rd Street. When a thin, dark-skinned man suddenly rushed up to the passenger side and tapped on the window, Coopersmith turned to look at him.

"Can you spare some change, Mister?"

"It's him," Coopersmith blurted out, just as the light turned green.

The driver of the car behind him sounded his horn and the man reacted by backing away from Coopersmith's car.

Coopersmith moved forward across the intersection and pulled over to the side of the road. By the time he had made it back to the spot, the man had gone.

He couldn't have gone too far. Coopersmith strode down 33rd Street heading east. "You see a man walking in this direction?" he said to a little boy playing in his yard.

The little boy shrugged. "I don't know."

Coopersmith continued to the end of the street, then doubled back to the Boulevard. He walked south for two blocks, pausing briefly to question a homeless woman pushing a grocery cart, then returned to his car. After driving around the block a few times he finally gave up and headed back to his office. He'd try again tomorrow…maybe with the help of one of the men from the shelter.

Twenty-Six

It was a simple funeral, just as Brother James had said it would be. Two homeless people, a black man and a white woman, stood near the grave along with Brother James and a young priest who acted nervous, as though this was his very first funeral over which he had to officiate.

They were in the middle of reciting a prayer when Coopersmith quietly walked up and joined them. Brother James acknowledged him with a nod and afterwards, thanked him for attending.

Coopersmith walked back to his car. He spotted Elizabeth standing in the distance next to a tree. She had been crying.

"I'm surprised you came," Coopersmith said.

"I'm kind of surprised myself." She wiped away her tears with her hand. "At the last moment, I decided I wanted to be here. I did love my mother despite what you may think. Unfortunately I was so wrapped up in my own anger and resentment that I never reached out to her when she needed me most. The fact is, I've spent the greater part of my life feeling sorry for myself, and I'm not very proud of it."

"You came, and that's what counts."

"Thanks." She flashed a soft smile. "Are you always this understanding with people you don't know very well?"

"Let's just say I'm not one to judge. I've seen a lot and I've done a lot and in my business, well, it pays to keep an open mind." He paused when he saw her glance toward the workers as they lowered her mother's casket into the ground.

"I should've done more." She struggled to hold back her tears.

"Listen, I know a diner not too far from here. They make a pretty good cup of coffee."

She smiled at him. "I think I'd like that. Why don't I follow you? Just give me a second while I get myself together."

Millie recognized Coopersmith as he and Elizabeth entered the diner and took the second booth from the door. "Hi, Joe." She strolled up to them with a coffeepot in her hand.

"How you doing, Millie?"

She smiled. "Can't complain. Not that it would do any good. Can I pour you some coffee?"

"Sounds good…and also for my friend."

Millie poured the coffee and then excused herself to take an order from a couple at the booth next to them. "Just let me know if you want to order something."

"Well, you know why I showed up today, but you haven't told me why you did," Elizabeth said, tearing a packet of sugar and pouring its contents into her coffee.

"I almost didn't. When Brother James called and told me the location, I instinctively found an excuse for not being able to attend."

"I can understand that. You didn't know my mother."

"That's not the reason." He paused to steady his voice. "My wife…is buried in the same cemetery. It's hard enough for me to go there to put flowers on her grave every couple of months."

"I'm sorry. I didn't know."

"It's been five years, but it feels like yesterday." He changed the subject. "So, tell me. How long have you lived in Miami?"

"I was thirteen when my mother and stepfather decided to

move down here. We were living in Buffalo where most of my family is from. Sometimes I wish we had stayed there."

"Why is that?"

"I felt like I belonged there, not like here, where I'm just another transplanted Yankee. Being an only child, I kind of miss having my family…my aunts and uncles nearby. I visit them every year, but it's not the same."

"I know what you mean. I'm an only child myself. I was raised in Boston but I've been here so long that I don't know if I could ever leave. Wouldn't mind splitting the year, though—summers up north and winters down here. It would be like having your cake and eating it too."

"I like the comparison," she said with a grin.

They talked through a second cup of coffee followed by a light lunch and when they were through, Coopersmith did something he hadn't done in a long time.

"It's probably bad timing, considering why we're here," he said, "but can I…can I call you sometime? I know this little restaurant in the Keys—more like a glorified hole in the wall—where they make the best conch chowder in Florida and the best and only Margarita pie."

Elizabeth nodded and smiled. "You've got my number." She suddenly became serious. "I want you to know that I really appreciate what you've done. If it hadn't been for you, my mother would've ended up in a pauper's grave just because I was too hurt and stubborn to do anything about it." She attempted to smile again. "Margarita pie?"

"It's the owner's invention. It's basically a key lime pie with a little tequila thrown in before baking. Kind of makes sense when you think of it. Tequila-lime. They go together, don't they? The purists hate it, but it really isn't bad."

After leaving the diner, Coopersmith dropped by Dolores's house. He hadn't talked to Sarah in a while, and he wanted to break it to her in person about the possibility that he had spotted her father.

"It was him, all right." He leaned forward on the couch. "If the light hadn't turned green, I might've had a chance to talk to him."

"Maybe he's still in the area," Sarah said.

"I don't know, maybe. Homeless people are always being chased off, and a lot of them would rather keep moving than risk having the cops pick them up for vagrancy."

She stared at him. "You're going back there, aren't you?"

"I thought I might have one of the men from the shelter give me a hand. They know the streets and the hideouts and they trust each other, at least more than they would a guy like me. It's definitely worth a try. Oh, I almost forgot to show you." He reached into the pocket of his coat and pulled out the Preacher's photo. "Keep it," he said, handing it to her. "I've got an extra one."

Sarah looked at the photograph and after a few seconds reached up to wipe away a tear from the corner of her eye. "Part of me wishes I didn't have to do it…to meet him and talk to him about the past. But I think I'd regret it later in life if I didn't do it when I had the chance. I know he probably didn't love my mother, but that doesn't matter. He's still my father and nothing can change that."

Coopersmith hesitated. "Just keep in mind that if and when I find him, there's a chance he may not…"

"I know," she said, nodding. "I'm just hoping he'll at least be curious enough to see what I look like. By the way, I've kept Kate up-to-date on everything. We get along just great, though I get the impression that her husband, Sal, isn't too thrilled to have me as a sister-in-law."

"He'll come around. I'm sure it's still new to him."

"I hope so, but if not, well, I'm sure Kate and I will still be good friends."

Coopersmith walked slowly toward the door. "If I get lucky tomorrow, you'll be hearing from me." He crossed his fingers and held them up in the air. "Wish me luck."

Twenty-Seven

Sitting in his car half a block from the shelter, Coopersmith spotted the wino who gave him the tip about the Preacher's hangout. He was coming out of the building carrying a stuffed garbage bag slung over his shoulder.

Coopersmith got out of the car and walked up to him. "How's it going? I want to thank you for that tip you gave me the other day."

The wino looked at him as though he didn't know what he talked about.

"The Preacher, remember? You said he hung out at the park near Thirty-Sixth Street."

"Yeah, yeah." The wino nodded.

"Listen, how would you like to make a few extra bucks?" He reached into his pocket and pulled out a twenty-dollar bill and held it out for him. "I want you to help me find the Preacher. I ran into him near Thirty-Third Street and Biscayne, but he took off before I could talk to him."

"Sure, I'll help you find him," the wino said, reaching for the money.

"Not so fast. You'll get it *after* we're through looking for him."

When they got near the corner of Biscayne and 33rd Street, Coopersmith pulled over and dropped the wino off in front of a grocery store. "I'll pick you up in an hour. Just go out and walk around the area. If you run into other street people, ask them if they've seen him around."

The wino nodded and walked off into an alley next to the store.

Coopersmith drove away and cruised the Boulevard between 21st Street and 54th Street. He saw a few homeless black men, but none that looked like the Preacher. Finally he went back to where he had dropped off the wino and waited for him to appear.

After a long wait, he glanced in the left side mirror and saw the wino strolling up to the car.

"If you'd come five minutes later, I'd have been gone," Coopersmith said to him. "I said an hour, didn't I? Never mind. What'd you find?"

"There's an empty house back there on Twenty-Eighth Street. It's boarded up, but they found a way in through the back. I saw a guy coming out and I asked him about the Preacher. He hadn't seen him for a couple of days but he said the Preacher sleeps there off and on."

Coopersmith smiled and handed him a twenty-dollar bill. "Good work." He hesitated for a second, then gave him his business card with a beeper number and a two-digit code circled in red. "I really need to find him. It's worth a hundred dollars if you find him for me."

"For a hundred bucks, I'll find him, you can bet on it," said the wino with renewed enthusiasm.

"Don't let me down now," Coopersmith said, as he cranked up the engine. He made a U-turn and drove back to 28th Street to check out the boarded-up house, then turned around and headed back to his office.

Coopersmith was on the phone when Sal and two well-dressed men who looked like body guards, came in and made themselves comfortable.

"We'll just wait," Sal sat down across from Coopersmith and looked around the room.

"They had me on hold," Coopersmith put down the phone. "What can I do for you?" He eyed the two men.

"I checked you out," Sal said, speaking slowly for effect. "You're pretty good at what you do...and that's what worries me."

"What are you talking about?"

"I'm talking about the old bum, the one you're trying to find. When you first put Sarah and Kate together, I wasn't that wild about it, but I figured if it made Kate happy, what the hell? But then when Kate told me you were getting close to finding him, that's when I knew this thing was getting out of control."

"Sarah wants to meet her natural father. What's the big deal?"

"It's very simple. This fucking lowlife is not going to be my father-in-law. Am I getting through to you?"

"I hear you. But Sarah is my client and it's really up to her to..."

"Here's the deal. Ten grand...cash, right now. All you got to do is tell Sarah that you tried but you couldn't find him. If you want you can give it a couple of weeks to make it look good." He paused to let Coopersmith think about it. "So what do you say? Do we have a deal?"

Coopersmith shook his head. "Sorry, no sale. I've never lied to a client and I'm not about to now, not for ten grand or fifty grand or any amount."

"You surprise me, you know that?" Sal crossed his arms. "It's not like I'm asking you to do something illegal. So what is it? I really want to know."

"Look, I sleep pretty good and you want to know why? Because I don't owe anybody anything and nobody owes me anything. It's kept me from making a few extra bucks now and then, but like I said, I sleep well."

"For a guy who doesn't carry a piece, you've got balls for saying no to my very generous offer. But just to show you I'm an understanding guy, I'm going to forget we ever had this little meeting...and I would advise that you do likewise." He stood up to leave and the two thugs did the same. "If you change your mind, you know where to find me."

After the trio left, Coopersmith slumped down in his chair and breathed a long sigh. He knew Sal's reputation, and had a feeling he'd not heard the last from him.

Later in the day he called Elizabeth and got no answer. He tried again when he got home and got her answering machine. "Hi, Elizabeth, it's Joe Coopersmith. About that little place in the Keys…I wondered if maybe…"

"Hi, Joe," Elizabeth said, picking up the call. She sounded tense and a little mysterious. "I was going to call you later tonight. I didn't want to leave without saying good-bye."

"Sounds kind of final, almost like your weren't planning on coming back. What's going on?"

"It's my husband, my ex-husband. He's very ill and he needs me. I don't expect you to understand, but I feel I have to be with him. Tomorrow morning I'm taking the first flight to Dallas and I don't know when I'll be back."

"You're right. I don't understand. I just assumed that because you were divorced, he was out of your life."

"You deserve an explanation… I don't exactly know how to say this, but I still care about him. The reasons we got divorced are really complicated. He was much older than me and at the time it didn't matter. In fact it made it easy for me to love him because he didn't demand or expect anything. In a way, we were good for each other. I had this fear of physical intimacy and he was too old to express himself in that way. But he made me happy and for several years that's what kept us together."

"You're feeling sorry for him? Is that why you're going to him?"

"Maybe in a way I am. But that's not why I'm doing this. I'm doing it because he did so much for me, not just when we were married but afterwards. He was more than generous with me. He made certain I would live comfortably for the rest of my life. He didn't have to do that. But that's the kind of man he is." She paused. "If I didn't go, to be with him for whatever time he has left, I know it would haunt me forever. It's something I have to do, Joe. I hope you understand."

"You didn't have to explain any of this, but I'm glad you did. I guess…there's nothing more to say, is there?"

"No, I guess there isn't. Take care of yourself."

"You, too."

He hung up the phone, waited a few seconds, then picked it up again and dialed. "How's my favorite sister-in-law?" Coopersmith said when he heard Laura's voice.

"Joe, what a surprise. Everything okay?"

"Couldn't be better. Just thought I'd call to see how you and Bill and the kids were doing."

"Everyone is doing fine. Bobby is just getting over a cold, the third one this year, and Rhonda, well she's six going on sixteen. She suddenly decided that she wants to be an astronaut. Yesterday it was a nun and the day before…well, you get the picture."

"Just be grateful she doesn't want to be a private eye. Wouldn't that be something?"

Laura chuckled. "That'll be next, mark my words. Listen, why don't you come over for dessert? I'd invite you for dinner, but we're just finishing up. The kids would really love to see you."

"If you're sure it isn't too late…"

"Of course not. I can show you some pictures we just got developed. The ones we took the last time you came for dinner. There's a really good one of you and Bobby arm wrestling on the floor."

"I'll be there in twenty minutes." He felt a little better. For a second he worried that maybe Laura had detected something wrong, and the invitation was her way of letting him know she understood. Not that it mattered. He needed to be with people he knew, and Laura and her family fit the bill perfectly.

Twenty-Eight

The Fixer acted bored as he nursed a bourbon on the rocks, his third in almost two hours. He was there for a purpose, and the sight of Sherri L'Amour shaking her tight little butt before a bunch of loudmouthed, horny guys—not exactly his idea of a good time.

"Another bourbon?" asked the nice-looking blond behind the bar. She looked like she had once been a stripper, maybe nine or ten pounds ago.

"I'm okay," he said curtly.

"This is about the third day in a row you've come in here," she said with a friendly smile. "Somehow I wouldn't peg you as a regular. You're not one of those mixed-up gays trying to decide which way to go, are you?" She grinned to let him know she kidded around.

He looked her over. "Why don't you meet me in the john and find out for yourself?"

"*Touché*," she said, the grin still on her face. "Sure you don't want another drink?"

"Thanks, but I think I'll call it a night." He downed the last of his bourbon and moved to step off the stool. He paused when he looked across the room and saw a man fitting Jerry's description walk in the lounge. "Maybe I will have another drink after all," he said, turning back toward the bar.

It was almost 1:00 a.m. when Jerry left the Body Double, got into his car, and headed north on Dixie Highway.

The Fixer didn't lag far behind. When he saw Jerry slowing down for a red light at 95th Street, he pulled alongside and jabbed a .40 caliber Glock pistol in Jerry's direction. He fired five shots in rapid succession and then waited for a second, as if to make sure the bullets had hit their mark.

As he sped from the scene, he felt a sudden rush, a kind of morbid euphoria which would last well into the next day and sometimes even the day after that.

Back at the light, Jerry's car had veered to the left, hitting a parked car and the front of a video store. Miraculously, Jerry was still alive, though just barely. He had taken three hits, one to the jaw, one to the neck, and the other just above his shoulder. When paramedics arrived four and a half minutes later, they found him still conscious. He was going into shock. He murmured, "Don't let me die. Don't let me die."

Eight hours later, Jerry still hung on. Emergency operations had saved him. For how long, no one could say.

Twenty-Nine

It was the kind of lead Coopersmith liked to handle personally: a quick interview to get a few facts followed by a call or a fax to the client, or in this case another private investigator, to report the results. He had gotten a fax from a private investigator in Minneapolis, a former FBI clerk that he didn't know but who had been referred to him by a mutual buddy, Ray Difalco.

On his way to cover the lead, Coopersmith went over the fax.

Background:

A thirty-year-old woman named Karen Ramsey recently committed suicide by taking an overdose of sleeping pills. When friends discovered her body, they found the wadded-up business card of a Miami psychiatrist named Ronald Erskine next to the empty bottle of pills. His address is 444 Brickell Avenue, suite 1501, Miami, Florida. Karen used to live in Miami but moved to Minneapolis a little over a month ago.

Her parents basically want to know if Erskine knew Karen. Was she his patient, friend or what? Because she left no suicide note, they are desperate to find some answers about what may have caused her to go over the edge.

If you have any questions call me, otherwise I'll wait to hear from you after you've conducted the interview.

Coopersmith had never met a psychiatrist before. He had this picture in his mind of a guy with a beard, wearing glasses and stroking his chin every time you asked a question. After waiting for almost an hour, he was surprised that he looked very ordinary—no beard, no glasses, no thoughtful gestures, and much younger than expected. Kind of reminded him of an unassuming banker or maybe even a lawyer.

"I want to thank you for seeing me without an appointment." Coopersmith took a seat on a small couch across from Dr. Erskine's desk. "I know you're busy, so I'll try to be brief."

Dr. Erskine glanced at the clock on his desk. "Yes, I would appreciate it. I have a patient scheduled in five minutes. So tell me, what is it you want to speak to me about? My secretary mentioned you had some news about a possible patient of mine?"

"Her name is Karen Ramsey. Do you know her?"

"She…was my patient a couple of years ago," he said reticently. "What about her?"

"Someone found her dead in her apartment in Minneapolis… along with your card next to an empty bottle of sleeping pills."

He looked truly stricken. "She committed suicide?"

"It looks that way. Too bad. She was only thirty years old."

"Did…she leave a note?"

Coopersmith shook his head. "That's why I'm here. Her parents were hoping you might know something. Something that could explain why she took the ultimate solution, so to speak."

"I'm afraid I really can't help you. As you know, there is the patient-doctor confidentiality consideration which prevents me from discussing her case with anyone, even her parents. I will say this, however—during the time she was my patient, I saw no indication that she was suicidal or that she even had thoughts along those lines. If her parents wish to call me, I will be happy to accept their call, but I won't be able to tell them much more than I've told you today."

"Why did she come to you in the first place?"

"I'm sorry, but I can't divulge that without…"

"I understand," Coopersmith said. "I hoped to leave here with a little more than what you've given me, but I can see it's not going to happen." He got up to leave and paused when he spotted a framed poster for a Miccosukee Festival hanging on the wall. The portrait of an unsmiling Indian dressed in native costume suddenly brought back memories. "I was there," he said, without facing Dr. Erskine. "All the years I lived in Miami I never gave the Miccosukees a second thought. I don't why, exactly. The village is just off the Tamiami Trail, not far from the city limits. Have you been to one of their festivals?"

"No, I never have. As a matter of fact I don't think I've even seen a Miccosukee Indian, but then again I wouldn't know what one looked like."

"Well, they look like him," Coopersmith said, pointing to the face on the poster. He caught an impatient look from Dr. Erskine. "By the way, what did Karen look like? Attractive?"

Caught a little off guard, Dr. Erskine said, "She was pretty, but not exceptional. Why do you want to know?"

"Just curious." He thanked him, left his office, and drove back to his own office to give the investigator in Minneapolis a call.

"That's about it," Coopersmith said, winding up his telephonic report. "If you want I can stay on it a while longer and see what else I can dig up. Maybe talk to some of her friends. I have a hunch Doctor Erskine was holding back on me for reasons that had nothing to do with her being his patient."

"I think what you've done is enough for now. I'll talk to the clients and see what they want to do. I get the impression they don't have the money to pay for a longer investigation on this, but you never know."

"Well, if you need me, you know where to reach me. If I don't hear from you within the next couple of days, I'll assume the clients don't want to pursue this further and I'll just send you an invoice."

"Fair enough," said the investigator. "In case I don't talk to you again, thanks for the fast response."

Coopersmith didn't recognize the voice or the name at first until she mentioned where she worked. She was Traci Lopez, Dr. Erskine's secretary.

"I need to see you, Mister Coopersmith." Her tone sounded urgent and a bit mysterious. "It's about Karen Ramsey. Where can I meet you?"

Coopersmith thought about it for a moment "How about the lobby of the Brickell Plaza hotel? Say…in forty-five minutes?"

"Make it an hour."

"I'll be there."

Coopersmith got to the hotel ten minutes early and took a seat in the lobby. He waited almost a half hour before she finally appeared.

"I didn't think you were going to show." He stood to greet her. She had on large sunglasses that made her petite face look even smaller.

"I'm sorry I'm late." She removed her glasses. "I had to make some last-minute calls for him."

When they were seated, Coopersmith studied her closely. "What's all the mystery about?"

"After you left the office, Doctor Erskine told me about Karen's suicide and he asked me to pull out her file, which I did. A few minutes later, I heard the shredder going and knew he was destroying the file. That's when I decided that I couldn't stand by and do nothing. Mister Coopersmith, I'm certain that if Karen committed suicide, it was because of Doctor Erskine and the things that went on between them."

"Were they having sex?"

"Yes, but it was much more than that. He abused his position and took advantage, not only of Karen but of other women. Women who were vulnerable, who were easily flattered and who trusted him with their innermost secrets."

"That's quite an accusation. How do you know so much about what went on between him and his patients?"

"I've been his secretary for seven years. I've met all his patients and I've typed and read almost everything in the files. More than once, women left his office crying and looking disheveled. It didn't take a rocket scientist to know what was going on in there."

Coopersmith looked around to make sure they weren't being overheard. "Tell me about Karen. Why do you think she took her life?"

"Karen was a very nice girl. A little shy, perhaps, but basically a normal person…that is, until she met Doctor Erskine. What I'm telling you is what Karen herself told me, and I had no reason not to believe her. He met her in a singles club along with other young women. His line, for lack of a better phrase, was to offer her a free psychoanalysis session. To Karen, and others like her, it was more like a game, and so she accepted. What did she have to lose, right?"

"Nothing but her life," Coopersmith said sarcastically.

Traci nodded sadly. "Well, from there, they were hooked, so to speak. Sometimes he offered them a follow-up session—free, of course—and after that they officially became fee-paying patients. Karen was typical. After three or four sessions, he convinced her she suffered from a form of latent nymphomania, which is bunk. I think he coined the phrase to suit his sick little scheme. Anyway, Karen eventually fell in love with him, which was the reason Doctor Erskine dropped her as a patient. He still saw her from time to time out of the office, and I can only guess what things he filled her head with." She paused and sighed. "He played with her mind and her heart, and then when it was no longer fun he threw her away like a tattered doll that's been sewn and patched up too many times."

"You obviously feel very strongly about this and I admire you for coming forward, but why didn't you do it sooner?"

"I'm a single mother with two kids and I was afraid of losing my job. I made more money than I've ever made in my life and I had to consider my kids before anything else. I know it's a poor excuse, but under the circumstances I thought I had no choice."

"You know I'm going to have to repeat what you've told me to State investigators."

"It won't be necessary. Before calling you, I made an appointment to meet with investigators from the Florida Board of Medicine. I know it'll be the end of my job, but after what happened to Karen, it's the least I can do." Her lips quivered and she added tearfully, "If I had come forward earlier, maybe Karen would still be alive."

On his way to his office, Coopersmith thought about everything Traci Lopez had told him and he asked himself if Karen's parents would be better or worse for knowing the whole sordid story about Karen and her psychiatrist lover. By the time he pulled into the parking lot, he had answered the question. He wouldn't be calling Minneapolis any time soon.

Thirty

When his beeper went off, Coopersmith rolled over and looked at the clock on his nightstand. It was one o'clock in the morning. Half asleep, he reached for his beeper. He recognized the double seven code he had assigned the wino, and jumped out of bed and dialed the number.

"Hello," said the wino. His voice sounded hoarse and indistinct.

"It's me, Coopersmith. What did you find?"

"The Preacher is at the house…the one I told you about. I don't know how long he's going to be there, so you'd better hurry. And don't forget the hundred dollars."

"Meet me at the corner of Thirty-Third Street and Biscayne. I'll be right there."

From a distance, Coopersmith could see the wino sitting on the curb. He gripped a bottle wrapped in a paper bag.

When he saw Coopersmith drive up and park just ahead of him, he took a long swig, then set the bottle down on the curb. He stood up and staggered toward Coopersmith's car.

"You got the hundred bucks?"

"You sure he's there?" Coopersmith climbed out of his car.

"He's there all right. I even talked to him, but I didn't tell him you were looking for him."

"Good, let's walk over there and if he's there you can take off."

The wino led the way to 28th Street and to the alley that ran behind the boarded-up house. When they reached the backyard, the wino said, "Wait here while I go in and get him. They don't like strangers coming into their little hideout, especially at this time of night."

Coopersmith didn't say anything as the wino climbed in through a narrow space between two boards that covered the window. Five minutes later, the man crawled back out through the same opening.

"Well, where is he?"

"He wants to know if you're a Christian. He won't talk to you unless he knows you're a Christian. I told you he was a little off in the head."

"I don't believe this shit." Coopersmith shook his head. "I want you to go back in there and tell him…oh, what the hell, tell him I'm the biggest Christian you ever met. And if it helps any, tell him that I go to church every Sunday." It was a lie; he hadn't seen the inside of a church in over a year. He would have said anything to get the Preacher to come out.

The wino went back into the house and after a couple of minutes, came out with the Preacher right behind him. His gaunt, dark face barely visible in the moonless night, the Preacher was cautious and hesitated for a moment.

"My name is Joe Coopersmith and I'd like to talk to you," Coopersmith stepped toward the Preacher. The wino, anxious to leave, distracted him. He pulled out a hundred-dollar bill and shoved it into the wino's shirt pocket.

The wino took a second to look at it, as if to make sure it was real, and then took off down the alley toward the Boulevard.

"What I have to talk to you about is very important," Coopersmith said. "Do you mind if we go somewhere else, maybe a coffee shop nearby?"

The Preacher tugged at the lapel of his dark, wrinkled jacket, which had a strong odor of dry perspiration. "I don't talk to people who aren't Christians. You sure you're a Christian?"

"Didn't the man tell you? Of course I'm a Christian…and I go to church every Sunday."

The Preacher thought about it for a long moment. "Okay, I'll talk to you."

When the waitress reached across to pour the Preacher some coffee, he waved her off. "Don't like it, never have, never will," he said without looking at her.

"Would you care for something else?"

The Preacher shook his head.

Coopersmith waited for the waitress to walk away and then started by making small talk, like Brother James had suggested. When he noticed the Preacher getting anxious, he hesitated for a second, then came right out with it.

"There's a woman—her name is Sarah Baker—who would very much like to meet you. I know her name doesn't mean anything to you, but she hired me to…"

"I used to know a Sarah. She was a good woman and a good Christian, too."

"Yes, I'm sure," Coopersmith said. "Like I said, Sarah hired me to find her natural family. Does the name Rebecca Longwood mean anything to you?"

"Rebecca Longwood. No. Who is she?"

"Maybe if I give you some background, it might jog your memory a little."

"My memory is just fine," the Preacher replied. "Why, I can remember when I was little boy. I used to be a bootblack, the best for miles around. I've been on my own since the age of twelve, you know."

"Getting back to Rebecca. Maybe you remember a man who took care of her for a while. Doc Morgan. He had a place near the Tamiami Trail."

Doc's name seemed to strike a nerve. "How come you know so much about Doc? He was good to me and he was good to Becky. We're going back many years now."

"Becky? Is that what she went by? Then you *do* remember her?"

"Of course I remember Becky. Becky was a sweet girl and she was nice to me. What a shame when she…"

"When she died in the old shack," Coopersmith said. He waited for a moment, then said, "Becky was Sarah's mother."

"I think I've heard enough. Someone obviously told you about Becky, Doc, and the things that went on back then. But that was before I became a Christian and I don't have to think about it anymore." He jumped up and left the table. He shook his head and mumbled to himself.

"We haven't finished talking," Coopersmith said, following him.

The Preacher ignored him as he exited the restaurant and stepped up his pace to get away from him.

"Sarah is your daughter," Coopersmith yelled out to him.

The Preacher stopped in his tracks and turned around slowly. "I figured that out. What do you want from me?"

"I know how uncomfortable you must feel about the way it happened back then, but you don't have to talk about it if you don't want. I just want to know if you would be willing to meet your daughter, Sarah. Regardless of how it happened, you're her father and she's your daughter. It doesn't have to be a long meeting—ten, fifteen minutes. It's up to you. Aren't you just a little curious to see what she looks like?"

The Preacher thought about it. "I didn't always live on the streets. I even got married once. People see us on the street and they think we have no feelings, that we don't care about things. But we do, some of us more than others."

"I think I know what you're trying to say," Coopersmith said, nodding. "It doesn't matter to Sarah that you live the way you do. She's not a judgmental person."

"Is she a Christian?"

"As a matter of fact, she is," Coopersmith said without

hesitation. He would have said anything to make him agree to a meeting. "So what's it going to be? Can I tell her that you're ready to meet her?"

"You know she means nothing to me, don't you?" the Preacher asked. "It's important she knows that. Something else. After we meet, she's got to promise she'll leave me alone. I don't want to hear from her or anyone else from those days."

"I'll make sure Sarah understands how you feel. Where would you like to meet?"

"At the shelter."

"How about tomorrow afternoon between three and four?"

"Not tomorrow. It's too soon. Make it in a couple of days."

"Okay, it's settled," Coopersmith said. "The day after tomorrow, without fail."

"I'll be there," said the Preacher as he abruptly turned and walked away, disappearing into an alley.

Walking back to his car, Coopersmith couldn't shake the feeling that he had met or seen the Preacher before. Was it from an old dog case from the past? Maybe. But at three in the morning he wouldn't strain his brain any more than he had to. Not when he had really important things to do, like get his sleepy ass back into bed where it belonged. If he were lucky, he had three, maybe four more hours of sleep.

Later in the morning, the Fixer flipped through the paper and spotted the article. His eyes moved quickly, scanning it. The doctors said the operations were successful and he had at least a fifty-fifty chance of making a full but slow recovery.

"I don't fucking believe it." The Fixer threw the paper across the room. "Three direct hits and the bastard is still alive."

He was still fuming when the phone rang. Mel hadn't heard from him since the day of the hit.

"I'm afraid we have a problem," said the Fixer. "The son of a bitch is still breathing."

"You mean he didn't die?"

"It happens sometimes. But don't worry, I'll fix it—at no extra cost."

"You said it would be a piece of cake. When the cops figure out…"

"I *said* I would fix it. I'll call you when it's over and done with. Just have my fee ready like we agreed." He hung up without giving Mel a chance to reply.

Thirty-One

"We have to talk." Sarah opened the door still wearing her robe and looking as though she hadn't slept well. Coopersmith followed her to the kitchen, sat down at the table, and waited for her to pour him some coffee.

"You found him, didn't you?" She poured herself a cup and sat across from him.

Coopersmith nodded. "I got a call in the middle of the night and I went out to see him. He was pretty typical of other homeless men I've met before. What surprised me, though, his mind was sharper than most and he had a good memory, too. But he's got this crazy thing about religion. Won't talk to anyone unless they're a Christian."

"Does he want to meet me?"

"The day after tomorrow. I tried to make if for today, but he said it was too soon. He'll meet us at the homeless shelter between three and four."

"Do you really think he'll show up?"

"I think so. I think he'll be there because he wants to get it over with. He's not looking forward to it, that's for sure. In fact, he made it very clear that after the meeting he doesn't want to see you again. I'm sorry to be so blunt, but that's what he said. Maybe after he gets to know you, he'll change his mind. For now I think you should look at it as a onetime thing."

"I'm glad you told me. At least I'll know what to expect." She paused. "What was he like? Did he…tell you about my mother?"

The meeting fresh in his mind, Coopersmith repeated everything they said. When he finished, he drank his coffee and then abruptly changed the subject. "There's…something else we need to talk about. I know you and Kate have been getting along pretty good. And you talk to each other a lot, don't you?"

"What are you trying say? Is there a problem?"

Coopersmith looked at her for a moment. "I wasn't going to tell you, but Sal paid me a visit the other day. He was concerned that when I found your father, he would suddenly have a homeless derelict as a father-in-law. He offered me ten grand to drop the search, using a suitable excuse, of course."

"I-I don't know what to say," Sarah stammered. "It's true that I've told Kate almost everything we're doing. And she probably mentioned it to Sal, not that it was any big deal, until now. I think I'll call Kate and tell her what Sal tried to do behind her back."

"No, it's better you leave it alone. I'd hate to give Sal and his goons a reason to drop by my office again. Just do me a favor and keep your conversations with Kate to non-family things or whatever else sisters talk about."

"Okay, if you think that's best. If she asks, I'll just say you've hit a dead end or something. I hate to lie to her, but I guess we have no choice, at least not until after I meet my father."

"Before I forget, I told your father that you were a Christian. So if he brings it up, you'll know how to play along."

Sarah chuckled. "Well, I am a Christian. Maybe not the kind he has in mind. But anyway, thanks for letting me know."

Back in his office, Coopersmith took his time listening to his phone messages while he went through his mail. When he heard a strange message from a Nurse Barker, he put down a letter he was reading and listened closely.

"I work at the ICU at Jackson Memorial Hospital. There's a man named Jerry brought in with gunshot wounds from which he may or may not recover. He gave me your name and phone number and requested that you come to see him as soon as possible.

He said something about Sarah and the briefcase, if that means anything to you. Anyway, you can call me or you can come to the hospital any time between eight in the morning and six in the afternoon."

He grabbed the newspaper from on top of his desk and flipped through the pages. "There it is," he said, slapping the back of his hand against the article. The caption read: MAN IN CAR SHOT BY UNKNOWN ASSAILANT. He finished reading the story on the way out the door.

The Fixer put on his coat, adjusted his collar, then walked over to the mirror on the wall. He smiled, envisioning himself dressed as a priest.

When he got to the hospital, the Fixer spent the first few minutes observing Jerry's room. He waited till it was safe and strolled in, closed the door behind him, then went straight to the bed where Jerry lay. He was about to disconnect the I.V. to Jerry's arm when Jerry awoke and saw what was happening. He tried to call for help, but was too weak to form the words. The Fixer took a small pillow and held it over Jerry's mouth, then quickly removed it when he heard voices and footsteps approaching.

"I must caution you, Mister Coopersmith, that he can't talk very well because of his wounds and the strong medication," Nurse Barker said. "But he can whisper a little, so you'll have to get close to him to understand what he's saying. He lapses in and out of consciousness throughout the day. Hopefully he'll be alert when you try to talk to him. Unfortunately, he hasn't given us much information and he refuses to cooperate with the police." She opened the door to the room and walked up to Jerry's bed.

Jerry's eyes widened, and he tried to speak and raise his arm.

"Well, I see that he wants to say something to you, so I'll leave the two of you alone," she said. "If you need me, I'll be down the hall."

"Thanks, I really appreciate it." He waited until he saw the door close behind her and then stepped up to the bed. "Jerry, listen to me. Who shot you? Did it have anything to do with the information in the briefcase?"

Jerry opened his mouth to try to speak and Coopersmith leaned closer. "What? I'm sorry, but I can't understand you. Try it again, but try not to rush your words."

"Hees heer, hees heer," Jerry whispered, frantic to make himself understood.

Coopersmith shook his head. "I still can't make it out. What is it you're trying to say?"

Jerry tried to raise his arm again, but couldn't. Then he tried to speak, but it came out garbled.

"Look, it's no use. I can't make out what you're saying. I'm going to leave for a while, but I'll be back later and we'll try again." As he turned to step away, his eye caught the refection of a silver crucifix, partially hidden between the folds of the sheet that covered the bed. He picked it up, looked at it briefly, and put it in his pocket. Then he stepped away and left the room.

"How did it go?" asked Nurse Barker, standing behind the nurse's station

"Not well. Couldn't make out anything he said, except maybe the last couple of words. It almost sounded like he said, 'Help me.' Doesn't make sense."

"Well, like I told you, he's very heavily medicated and it's probably a struggle for him."

"When do you think he'll get better? I mean, so I can understand what he tried to tell me."

"His doctor is probably going to adjust his pain medication, so I'd say you can come back later tonight or to be on the safe side, tomorrow morning."

Coopersmith thought about it as he rubbed the back of his neck. "He had this look on his face like he was desperate. I think I'll be back tonight. Oh, I almost forgot." He reached into his pocket and pulled out the silver crucifix. "I found it on his bed. Maybe one of the nurses dropped it there."

"Well, it's not Jerry's, I can tell you that. Why don't you leave it with me? I'll make sure it gets to its rightful owner."

From the corner of his eye, Coopersmith caught a glimpse of a priest walking past them toward the elevator. "Maybe it belongs to him," Coopersmith said. He called out to him, trying to catch his attention. "Father. I think this belongs to you."

The priest turned to look at Coopersmith, then turned back around and started running down the hall, nearly tripping as he pushed away an old man in a wheelchair.

"Damn it. Jerry tried to tell me something but I couldn't understand," he said, rushing down the corridor to get to Jerry's room.

"What are you talking about?" Nurse Barker followed right behind him.

Too late. Jerry was already dead.

"Oh, my God," she gasped.

"Call the police," Coopersmith hollered as he ran out of the room to try to catch up with the bogus priest.

He got to the parking lot just in time to see the man speeding away in a dark blue Blazer. He ran to his own car parked near the exit and took off after him.

The Blazer sped toward the onramp to the expressway. Coopersmith gained on him, running a red light, cutting in and out of traffic and blasting his horn at every car in front of him.

By the time Coopersmith reached the expressway, the man had stretched his lead, barreling north along the fast lane at more than 80 miles an hour. Coopersmith could barely see him and was tempted to call it off. Too dangerous. Just as he started to pull back a bit, the man sideswiped a yellow Cadillac, causing it to veer into the path of a fast-moving van. The driver of the van had little time to react and slammed into the rear of the Cadillac which spun out of control and into the path of yet another car traveling in the same direction.

In the distance, the Blazer shrank to just a speck of blue, and then it disappeared completely. Coopersmith returned to the hospital, gave a statement to the police, and then went back to his office. He called Larry McCaffee in Mobile to let him know what happened. He also called Sarah.

"We don't chose our parents," she said, after a long silence, "but we can make the best of it when things don't turn out the way they should. Too bad Jerry didn't see it that way instead of trying to get back at our mother's memory. That's what he was doing, you know, and he probably didn't even realize it. But maybe he did. I guess we'll never know."

"I guess not," Coopersmith said. "About tomorrow's meeting…"

"Can you pick me up around two fifteen?"

"You got it. And remember, you're a church going Christian," he said, trying to end the conversation on a lighter note.

The next morning, Coopersmith got a call from the detective he had met at the hospital. He was calling from Jerry's motel room which he and his men had just finished searching.

"Couldn't find that briefcase you said contained all those papers. Any chance the bogus priest might have taken it?"

"It's possible, I suppose," Coopersmith said, after considering it for a moment. "By the way, don't forget the name I gave you, Hal Brewster. If I were a betting man, I'd put my money on him being behind Jerry's murder."

"Yeah, well, it's going to take a lot more than a bet to tie him to the guy who did this job. I'd appreciate it if you keep in touch and let me know if you hear anything. I have a feeling we're going to need a lot of luck on this one."

"Sure. Whatever I pick up you'll be the first to know." He knew the detective was right. Without a good tip or an unexpected break, Jerry's murderer would never see the inside of a courtroom.

Thirty-Two

Coopersmith and Sarah arrived at the shelter a few minutes early and sat in the car for a while, then went inside and talked with Brother James, who had been expecting them.

"I'm supposed to be at a fundraiser in Coral Gables in twenty minutes. But you're welcome to stay in my office as long as you like. If you need anything, one of the volunteers will be glad to help you."

"Thanks," Coopersmith said. "We'll be all right."

"Good luck, Sarah," Brother James said, hurrying out of the office. "I'll say a little prayer for you and your father."

Sarah smiled. "Thank you."

"Can I get you something, some coffee or a cold drink?" Coopersmith asked.

"No, thanks." She looked up at the clock on the wall. "It's almost three o'clock. Do you think he'll be on time?"

"He'll be here. My guess is he's probably on his way. Wouldn't be surprised if he walked in the door any minute now."

It was almost four-thirty and the Preacher had yet to show. "If he were coming, he would've been here by now." Coopersmith got up and paced. "I just can't understand it. He really seemed sincere."

"Why don't we give him another ten minutes? Maybe he got the time wrong or maybe…"

"I have an idea. Let's go out to the place on Twenty-Eighth

Street. It beats sitting here doing nothing."

"Might as well." Sarah grabbed her purse.

They drove over to the house on 28th Street, which had a FOR SALE sign that hadn't been there before. After going around the back and looking through all the windows, they called the realtor from a nearby pay phone and found out that the cops had cleared the place out. Starting tomorrow morning, the house would be fixed up and remodeled.

Back to square one, Coopersmith thought as he took Sarah back to her place.

Returning to the shelter to see if anyone had seen the Preacher, he ran into the wino as he came out, and took him aside. "Listen, the Preacher was supposed to have been here a while ago. You haven't seen him, have you?"

"Not since the night I called you. Did you try the house where he slept?"

"The cops ran everybody out of there. The place is empty."

The wino scratched his scraggly beard. "For another hundred bucks I'm sure I could find him again."

"You're on. Call me the minute you see him."

A week later, Coopersmith had not heard from the wino nor from Brother James, who had promised to keep an eye out for the Preacher. On his way to interview a new client, he dropped by Dolores's place to talk to Sarah about the possibility that her father may have moved away from the area.

Sitting across from her in the living room, he could tell she'd been crying.

"I can come back another time."

"That's all right. As a matter of fact I'm glad you're here. You and Dolores are about the only ones I can count on when things get heavy like they did early this morning."

"Mark again?"

Sarah nodded. "He called me, just to talk, like he does every now and then. When I told him I had gone to the shelter to meet my father, he suddenly became quiet and then he said something really horrible, which I don't even want to repeat. Then he gave me an ultimatum. Either I stop trying to see my father or he would file for divorce. That's the first time he ever put it that way, and it made me question whether I ever really knew him. I mean, when I first met him, he was so charming, so thoughtful. He even sent me a white rose every day for the entire week just before we were married."

"I don't know about roses, but I do know people," Coopersmith said. "Mark strikes me as the kind of guy who does all the right things for the wrong reasons and sometimes the wrong things for no reason at all. In other words, he's confused and he may snap out it. But then again…" He shrugged and shook his head.

"You don't think very much of him, do you?"

"I didn't say that. Besides, it's not my place to express an opinion about a client's spouse. I'm just sorry things haven't gotten better between the two of you."

"Well, he's made it very clear how he feels and he's put the ball squarely in my court. Dolores thinks I should call his bluff and get it over with. Maybe she's right. But still, when I think of the good times…well, it's not easy chucking eight years of marriage, no matter what the reason."

"Before I forget, the medical examiner is releasing Jerry's body to a local funeral home hired by your cousin Cassandra. Apparently she's planning on having the body shipped up to Mobile for burial there. I just thought you'd want to know."

"I'm glad you told me. I only talked to her that once after you gave me her number. She seemed very nice, even invited me to fly up there to spend a few days with her. Maybe I'll call her and see if there's anything I can do. After all, he *was* my brother."

"That might not be a bad idea. I mean, about you flying up there to get away for a few days. It'll give your husband a chance to cool off a bit and it'll help take your mind off everything that's been going wrong lately."

She nodded. "I do need a vacation. But I'd hate to miss what may be the only chance I'll get to meet my father. What if you find him and he wants to see me right away? After what happened—or rather, what didn't happen at the shelter—I'm not taking any chances. You think he's doing it on purpose, staying out of sight the way he's done the past week?"

Coopersmith thought about it. "I don't know, but I find it hard to believe that he changed his mind all of a sudden. Something spooked him at the last moment. But what? That's what we have to find out."

The phone rang and they both turned to look at it. "Excuse me a second." Sarah got up to answer it. It was Mark, and within seconds, her eyes filled with tears.

Coopersmith waited a moment, then got up and left the house.

The new client's place was across town just north of Miami Lakes. He had gotten a call the night before from a woman who didn't say much except that it concerned a delicate matter, which she didn't want to get into over the phone. When he got there half an hour later, he saw a police car parked in front, and wondered if her call to him had anything to do with it being there. He waited a few minutes then walked up to the house and rang the bell.

An attractive, dark-haired woman in her late thirties opened the door. "Mister Coopersmith?" she asked, extending her hand to him. "I'm Sylvia Mendez."

"How are you? Is everything okay?"

"I had a break-in early this morning, the second in less than a month." She invited him into the living room, where two policemen were getting ready to leave.

"Here's a copy of the report," said one of the cops, handing the paper to Mrs. Mendez. "You may want to think about investing in a good alarm system. It won't keep them out but it might scare them off, and it'll probably improve our response time."

"Thanks for the advice. I might just do that." The two policemen walked out of the house. She closed the door behind them and joined Coopersmith in the living room. "Please have a seat." She sat down across from him and picked up a cigarette from the table in front of her, lighting it. "You don't mind, do you?" She exhaled the smoke away from him.

"That's okay. I'm used to it."

"I know that you don't like to work domestic cases, but I hope you'll make an exception. In fact, it's a missing person case, in a way."

"The missing person wouldn't happen to be your husband, would it?"

"Well, he's not exactly missing, although I haven't seen him in weeks. To put it bluntly, he's avoiding me. Anyway, the delicate matter I mentioned to you last night has to do with my husband and our pending divorce. Last Thursday would've been our fifteenth anniversary. He's dumping me for a twenty-eight-year-old little tramp he's had on the side for over a year."

She paused to take a drag from her cigarette. "Before I go into the reason I called, there's something you should know about me, or rather about what happened to me thirteen years ago. That's when I caught my husband cheating on me for the first time. I was so angry I did something stupid. I cheated on him. It was a one-night stand with a guy from work who had always been nice to me. Afterwards, I knew I had made a mistake, and basically put it out of my mind. But then when I learned I'd gotten pregnant, I knew the father was not my husband. I wanted to tell him and should have, but I didn't…until three weeks ago. We were fighting about the divorce and I blurted it out."

"How did he take it?"

"Not very well. In wanting to get back at him, I only succeeded in making things worse. Since then, he has barely spoken to our son, Andrew, who can't understand why his father is being so cold to him. They used to be very close."

"I sympathize with your problem, but I'm not sure I understand what you think I can do for you."

"I was just getting to that. The divorce will soon be final; it's more important than ever that he not abandon his son. I may think he's the biggest rat that ever walked the earth, but I'm smart enough to know a son needs his father. I've tried calling him at his office, but he refuses to take my calls. I've even sent him two letters, which he returned unopened. That's when I decided I needed help. When I talked to my friend Elizabeth several days ago, she was very sympathetic and she said she knew someone who could…"

"Did you say Elizabeth?"

"Elizabeth Conners. I'm sorry, I thought I told you last night when I talked to you."

"No, you didn't. What did she tell you about me?"

"Not much. That you were a kind, compassionate man and you were good at getting people to talk to you."

"That's it?"

"You sound disappointed."

"No, I—just curious." He cleared his throat. "I'm sorry for interrupting. You were telling me why you think I can I help you."

She took another puff on her cigarette and exhaled slowly. "My son is having a birthday next week. If his father doesn't show up he's going to be absolutely devastated. Just this morning I tried calling my husband's office, without identifying myself, of course. The girl who answered said he had left town and wouldn't be back for a week or so. If I can't convince my husband to do the right thing for the sake of the son who has called him Daddy ever since he was born, well…I just don't know what I'm going to do." She paused to crush her cigarette in a crystal ashtray. "I called you because I thought you could do something, maybe act as a neutral go-between or whatever."

"You want me to talk to him about this? That's a pretty tall order. You said he had left town. Do you know where?"

Sylvia shook her head. "That's one of the things you'll have to find out. Will you do it?"

"Look, I have to be honest with you. From what you've told me, it will take more than a simple conversation to make him come to his senses. And that's if I'm lucky to even get close to him."

"You're my only hope, Mister Coopersmith. The way Elizabeth talked about you, well, I'm sure you're the right man for the job."

A long silence, and then, "Elizabeth must be a good friend of yours. We wouldn't want to disappoint her, would we?"

Sylvia smiled. She provided Coopersmith with everything he needed to know, including a recent photograph of father and son taken during a fishing trip in the Keys.

Coopersmith looked at the photograph, then dropped it into the pocket of his coat. "I'll call you as soon as I know something." He paused. "If you hear from Elizabeth, tell her I said hello."

From his office, Coopersmith called Peter Mendez's office, using the pretext that he was a businessman from New York. "It's very important I speak to him," he said with an urgent tone. "I've got some documents that have to be in his possession by tonight or tomorrow morning at the latest."

The secretary put him on hold and came back ten seconds later. "I'm sorry, but Mister Mendez is out of town. Won't be back until sometime next week. If it's an urgent matter, I can call him and relay a message."

"Look, if I had known he would be out of town I would've made other arrangements. Can't you give me an address where I can send them to him by overnight delivery?"

"I'd like to help you, but his instructions were very specific. The best I can do is to take your number and have him call you."

Coopersmith thought about it for a moment, then gave her his number and a false name. "I'll be expecting his call," he said, hanging up.

While he waited, he went over Sarah's file and called his friend at the morgue, a few cops he knew, and Ray Difalco. He hoped someone had read or heard something about the Preacher. They hadn't, but promised to call if anything developed.

It was almost seven o'clock and he still hadn't heard from Mendez. He'd give him ten more minutes and then he'd lock up and call his office again first thing in the morning. Exactly nine minutes later, the phone rang.

"Hello?"

"This is Peter Mendez. May I speak to Joe Johnson?"

"I'm sorry, you must have the wrong number." Coopersmith disconnected.

He glanced at the central Florida number on the caller I.D., waited a few seconds, then dialed. "Lake Wales Inn," said a friendly woman's voice on the other end.

"Oh, I'm sorry, I must have misdialed." He smiled and hung up.

Thirty-Three

Lake Wales was an easy four-hour drive up the turnpike, then west on Highway 60. If he were lucky, he'd be back in time for the six o'clock news.

Pulling into the parking lot of the Lakes Wales Inn, he looked across the long row of cars parked in front of each cottage and spotted Mendez's blue Volvo with a tag number that matched the one Sylvia Mendez had given him. He got out of his car, walked up to the cottage that had a DO NOT DISTURB sign hanging on the doorknob and knocked twice.

"Just a minute," said an irritated male voice from inside. A moment later, a short, beefy man, wearing a terry cloth robe opened the door. Over his right shoulder, Coopersmith caught a quick glimpse of a bare-breasted woman scurrying into the bathroom.

"I'm sorry to disturb you, but I wonder if I can speak to you for a moment. My name is Joe Coopersmith. I tried to reach you at your office, but your secretary said you were out of town."

"How did you know where to find me?" Mendez asked, suspiciously.

"It wasn't that hard. Look, it's really important I speak to you. If you want, I'll wait until you get dressed and we can talk at one of the tables by the garden."

"My wife sent you, didn't she? If it's about the divorce, you can tell her to go to hell." He stepped back to close the door.

"It's not about the divorce, it's about your son," Coopersmith shot back.

Mendez looked at him carefully. "Give me a minute."

Moments later they met in the garden. "I want you to know that I came to deliver a message, that's all." Coopersmith sat across from Mendez. "What you decide to do is your business."

"Get to the point. You said it was about my son. What's the message?"

Coopersmith hesitated. "Before I get to that, you should know your wife told me everything."

"She had no right to do that. It's a personal thing between us and I really don't have to discuss it with you or anyone else."

"You're right. The only problem is that your wife has been trying to reach you without success. It got to the point that she didn't know what else to do, so she hired me. Which brings me to the reason I am here." Coopersmith cleared his throat. "I'll come right to the point. Your son's birthday is next Wednesday and your wife was concerned that you weren't going to be there."

Mendez turned away for a moment. His jaw muscles tightened and he sighed as he turned back to look at Coopersmith. "I hadn't forgotten. But—how can I say this without sounding like a terrible father—I'm still trying to deal with the fact that he isn't my real son, my flesh, my blood. Maybe it's because I'm Cuban, I don't know. You see, Latins believe that when you marry a woman, she's supposed to be pure and good, just like our mothers were to our fathers. It's a cultural thing and it goes against everything I was taught to believe in. When my wife told me I wasn't Andrew's father, it was the worst possible thing she could've done to me. She could've taken my car, my home, my money, and it would have been nothing compared to what she did by taking away my pride in being Andrew's father."

"Would you rather she had kept it a secret…forever?"

Mendez thought about it. "I don't know. Sometimes I wish she had. Anyway, it doesn't really matter now, does it?"

"I guess not. The question is, do you want to punish your son for something over which he had no control?"

Mendez shook his head. "Of course not. I planned on calling him on his birthday just to let him know I hadn't forgotten."

"I'm glad you said that. Somehow I knew you'd want to wish him a happy birthday, although I'm sure it would mean a lot more to him if you were to do it in person."

Mendez looked down for a moment, then stood up. "I'll… think about it." He swallowed hard, turned, and walked away.

Coopersmith sat there for a moment, then found a pay phone near the office and dialed Sylvia's number.

"Hello?" Sylvia sounded as though she had been expecting his call.

"I'm in Lake Wales. Just finished talking to your husband."

"How did it go?"

"Hard to say. But I think he'll be there for Andrew's birthday."

"Did he actually say that?" She sounded hopeful.

"No, but I could tell that despite everything that's happened, he loves his son and he doesn't want to disappoint him."

"I don't know what to say. How can I thank you?" Her voice broke.

"You just did. I'll tell you all about it when I get back to Miami." He had a smile on his face as he pulled out of the lot and headed east toward the highway.

Thirty-Four

A week and a half later, Coopersmith had run out of leads. No one had seen or heard from the Preacher since the day before he was scheduled to meet Sarah at the shelter.

When a call from his friend, Marvin, at the morgue came in, Coopersmith held his breath and braced himself for the worst. He sighed as he listened to Marvin's description of a body that had just been delivered.

"The guy was found near a canal off Okeechobee Road west of Hialeah. Had three bullet wounds to the back of the head. He could be a dark Latino or maybe black. He's roughly about the same age as the guy you've been looking for."

"Can you tell how long he's been dead?"

"Hard to say until we do the autopsy. My guess is that it was a couple of weeks, maybe longer."

"Before you do anything, let me take a look at him. I'll be there as fast as I can." Coopersmith rushed out of the office.

"That's him, all right. He had on the same clothes when I met him."

"Looks like an execution," Marvin said, focusing on the wounds in the back of the man's head. "Any idea who could have done this?"

Coopersmith stepped back from the body and thought about it. "I didn't think the son of a bitch would go this far. If I had dropped the case like he wanted me to, the old guy would still be alive."

Marvin looked confused. "What are you talking about?"

"Nothing." Coopersmith stomped out of the room.

Coopersmith wanted to break the news to Sarah in person. When he got to Dolores's house, Dolores was home alone. Sarah had left to run an errand only moments before.

"You look like you just lost your best friend," Dolores said, her wet hair wrapped in a towel. "Want to come in?"

"Might as well." He stepped inside and sat down on the couch.

Dolores sat down across from him. "Bad news, I take it." She tightened the towel around her head.

"The worst. Sarah's father was found dead near a canal off Okeechobee Road."

"Oh, no," she gasped, covering her mouth with her hand. "Sarah is going to be devastated. What happened to him?"

"Someone put three bullets in the back of his head."

"But who would want to kill him? He was just a harmless old guy. They normally don't die that way, unless…"

"Unless someone decides that being down and out doesn't make for a very good in-law," Coopersmith said with a bitter tone.

"I don't get it."

Coopersmith looked at her, his eyes blazing. "I'm saying that Kate's good-for-nothing husband killed him, or had him killed. He offered me ten thousand bucks to drop the case just so he wouldn't have to worry about having the old guy as a father-in-law."

"Have you told the cops?"

"Not yet. I've got no proof. I may never find any. I was going to wait until Sarah got back, but maybe it's better if she heard it from a friend. Just do me a favor. After you tell her, don't repeat what I said about Kate's husband. It may be more than she can handle."

Dolores nodded. "You're probably right. But don't be surprised if she calls you. I'm sure she'll have a lot of questions."

"Well, if she does, I'll tell her what I know…which isn't much, I'm afraid."

When Coopersmith got beeped an hour later, he recognized Sarah's number and called her right back.

"I'm sorry I didn't get to tell you personally."

"We were so close to getting him to meet me. I just don't understand it. Who would want to do such a thing and why?"

"I…don't know. Maybe the police will find the killer. But it's not going to be easy, I can tell you that."

"You know something, don't you? When Dolores told me about it, I could tell she held back on something. What is it?"

"I wasn't going to say anything just yet, but since you brought it up…well, I think Sal had something to do with it. The only trouble is, there's no way to prove it."

"For Kate's sake I hope you're wrong. But if you're not, I probably share some of the blame for telling her too much about how close you were to finding my father."

"Are you going to be okay?"

"Yeah, I think so." She hesitated. "Can you find out what I have to do to claim the body? I'd like to take care of the funeral arrangements."

"I'll talk to the coroner and let you know sometime today or tomorrow. I'll also call Brother James. He can arrange to perform the services, unless you know of someone else."

"No, I think that's a good idea." Another long silence. "Well, I guess that's it." She tried hard not to cry. "The case is over and there's nothing more for you to do, is there?"

"I have to give you credit, Sarah. You saw it through to the end. Most people would've given up a long time ago. I'll be around if you need me."

Thirty-Five

Coopersmith didn't hear from Sarah for almost a month. When she called early one morning to find out if he'd heard from Daniel, he was reluctant to tell her.

"He's being released in a couple of days. But nothing has changed. He still doesn't want to meet you. That's why I didn't call you. His only plans are to visit your father's grave. As a matter of fact, I told him I'd meet him there Sunday morning at ten o'clock. I've got an idea. If you should just happen to be at the cemetery at the same time, well…"

Later, when Coopersmith picked up the phone, he smiled and leaned back in his chair. It was Elizabeth.

"I didn't expect to hear from you. Are you still in Dallas?"

"Unfortunately, yes. Jason passed away six days ago."

"I'm sorry."

"I'm still in kind of a daze. I've hardly slept since I got here. Maybe now I can get a little rest. I meant to call you earlier, but half the time I was too exhausted, running between his house and the hospital and having to constantly defend myself against things his children were saying about me. They were horrible. His oldest son called me a vulture, accusing me of being there just so I could get a bigger share of his father's money."

"Sounds to me like you're ready to come home."

"I was ready the day I arrived. But I'm afraid it's not going to be any time soon. His children are contesting his will, which made sure I'd continue to receive the same monthly stipend he had been sending me since our divorce three years ago. They've hired the best lawyers money can buy and so far they've managed to convince a judge that all current payments to me should be suspended until the case goes to court."

"So what are you going to do? These things take months, sometimes years. You might want to think about coming back here to regroup and figure out how you're going to fight this."

"They'd like nothing better than to see me pack up and leave. I wouldn't give them the satisfaction. Besides, the attorney I hired thinks it would best for me to stay put, at least until he's had time to write a few motions. I'm on their turf and a non-Texan to boot, which means that I might as well be from Bangladesh as far as Texas judges are concerned."

"Is there anything I can do?"

"Not really. But thanks for asking."

"Well, if you ever do need anything, I'm only a phone call away." He paused, suddenly nervous. "Can I call you sometime?"

"I'd like that. It'll be good to hear from a friendly voice for a change. I'm staying at the Royal Arms Hotel."

Coopersmith repeated the name as he jotted it down. "By the way, I'm still holding a rain check for that restaurant in the Keys."

"I'm looking forward to it." Her voice sounded light, almost cheerful. "I can't wait to try a piece of that Margarita pie you talked so much about."

Coopersmith's good mood faded when he read an in-coming fax from Difalco. He'd found out Sal Guadagno had been the prime suspect in the murder of a low-level mobster two years ago in West Palm Beach. Homicide detectives suspected that Sal and two of his men hacked up a rival hoodlum and thrown his body parts into an alligator-ridden canal. It turned out that a hunter killed an alligator from the same canal later in the day. The hunter sold it to a local tanner. When the tanner cut into the alligator, he was shocked to find a partially digested hand with a gold ring still on one of its fingers. The ring had the initials LG engraved on the inside, which the cops traced to a small-time hood named Lino "The Monkey" Graglia. Although no one could ever prove it, the word on the street was that Sal ordered the killing "for personal reasons."

Difalco advised him to be careful, to drop it and let the cops handle it, the sooner the better.

Coopersmith put the fax down, waited a couple of minutes, then left. Difalco was right…the guy was a killer, and he'd just as soon let the cops take it from here.

"That's about it in a nutshell," Coopersmith said a while later, sitting across from Detective Dave Sanchez. "If I had known how dangerous he really was, I'd have pulled out of the case and that would've been the end of it. Homeless man or not, the poor guy didn't deserve to die that way."

Detective Sanchez crossed his hands behind his head and leaned back in his chair. "This is not going to be easy, I can tell you that. Even the motive is a little weak. The guy offs the old man just because he doesn't want him as a father-in-law?"

"What about my conversation with him? He offered me big bucks to drop the search for the old man. I know it's not proof, but it sure makes for an awful coincidence that the Preacher was killed just a few days after our conversation."

"It's your word against his…and his two friends. Besides, he really didn't say much, at least nothing that would make a jury believe he would have committed murder if you didn't accept his offer."

Coopersmith clenched his jaw. "That son of a bitch is going to get away with murder. I knew it the moment I saw the old man's body lying in the morgue."

"We're going to do what we can, but you're right. He may get away with it unless someone comes forward, which I expect is not going to happen in a case like this."

"So what *are* you going to do?"

"Well, for starters, it'd be interesting to see what he tells you the next time you talk to him. You've been in this business long enough to know it's the only way."

"I hoped I wouldn't have to get involved," Coopersmith said. "What did you have in mind, a phone call?"

Sanchez nodded. "Give me a second while I call the state attorney's office to get their blessing." He picked up the phone and dialed a number.

While he waited, Coopersmith walked over to the drinking fountain across the room. As he leaned forward to take a drink, he spotted a Miccosukee tribe policeman standing next to the copying machine. He stared at him for a second as he finished taking a drink.

"Ready when you are," Detective Sanchez said in a loud voice.

Coopersmith walked back to Detective Sanchez's desk, picked up the phone with a recording device attached to it, and dialed Sal Guadagno's number. He let it ring six times, hung up and dialed again. Sal answered on the second ring.

"We need to talk," Coopersmith said.

"Who's this?"

"Coopersmith. You didn't have to kill him, for God's sake. The poor guy probably didn't have long to live."

"What the fuck are you talking about?" Sal asked.

"If I'd taken the ten grand, the old guy would still be alive. You probably could've bought him off and sent him to the other side of the country, did you ever think of that?"

"You've got balls, Coopersmith, I'll give you that. But I'll tell you again, I don't know what the fuck you're talking about. Do us both a favor. Don't call me again." He slammed the phone down before Coopersmith could ask another question.

"The guy was on to you right from the start," Detective Sanchez said, pressing the off button on the recorder next to the phone. "Well, we figured it wouldn't be easy."

"Yeah," Coopersmith said, nodding. "It's going to take more than a phone call, that's for sure." He reached to shake Detective Sanchez's hand. "You got my number. Call me if you come up with something."

"You can count on it. Thanks for the help."

As Coopersmith walked across the large, open squad area, he paused briefly to glance at the Miccosukee policeman. There was something about him, something about his deep-set eyes and dark features that reminded him of someone he knew or had met before.

Driving back to his office, Coopersmith couldn't get the Indian policeman's face out of his mind. If what he was thinking were true…

He spotted a pay phone up ahead and pulled over to make a call. "I'm glad I caught you at home," he said, recognizing Sarah's voice when she answered. "Listen, I have something I want to check out and I want you to come with me."

"What's this about?"

"I'll explain everything when I pick you up. I'll be there in half an hour."

"But…"

He had already hung up.

"You sounded very mysterious," Sarah said as she got into the car. "Do you mind telling me what's going on?"

Coopersmith backed out of the driveway and pulled away slowly. "A few weeks ago I saw a poster hanging on the wall of a psychiatrist's office. It was an ad for a Miccosukee Festival. I guess some people like to hang them up, like works of art, you know? Anyway, the poster had this portrait of an Indian…" He caught a puzzled look from her.

"Bear with me for a second," he said. "Well, the Indian's face stayed in my mind but I didn't know why exactly, until I saw a similar-looking face today at the Miami-Dade Police Department. Suddenly it all came together, sort of. You see, when I first met your brother Daniel, his looks surprised me. He really didn't look black, exactly. He looked, well, different in a way I couldn't explain, until now. Then, when I met your father, I didn't know what to make of him. I had a feeling I'd seen him before...and I had. Or at least someone who looked like him."

"You don't mean the picture in the poster?"

"Bingo. It obviously wasn't a picture of your father, but the features, the general characteristics—they were all there."

"Are you trying to say that my father was a...Miccosukee Indian and not a black man?"

Coopersmith slowed for a stop sign, nodding. "It's just a hunch, mind you, and there's a good chance I may be wrong. But I wanted you to be with me just in case."

"So where are we going?"

"Where it all began. On the Tamiami Trail. The Miccosukee village, to be exact."

An hour later, they arrived at the reservation. They turned into a small village surrounded by swampland and tall grass and parked in front of a wooden building which had a sign over the entrance that said: CURIOS, MOCCASINS, INDIAN JEWELRY.

"Let's go in and ask a few questions," Coopersmith said.

They got out of the car and walked into the shop, paused to look around, then approached a young woman behind the counter. She had the same eyes, the same cheekbones as Daniel and the Preacher.

"I wonder if you can help us," Coopersmith said with a smile. "We're...doing some research on the Miccosukee tribe and we were hoping to find someone who knows the history of the village, the way it was over sixty years ago."

The young woman smiled. "You need to talk to Grandma. She's not my Grandma, but that's what everybody calls her. She's been around forever. I don't know how old she is, but she's seen and done more than anybody else."

"Where can we find her?" Sarah asked.

"She lives down the road, the third house to the left. The one with an open hut next to it. She likes to sit out there for hours. But I warn you, she'll talk your ear off if you let her."

"Thanks," Sarah said. She followed Coopersmith out the door and hesitated. "This is crazy. I can't believe you talked me into coming here. What if the whole thing turns out to be a wild goose chase? What if…"

"You're right. This is a little crazy and maybe I should've checked it out on my own before telling you anything. But we're here, so what have we got to lose? If I'm wrong, and there's a fair chance that I am, I'll consider getting a new line of work."

"You don't have to go that far," she said, forcing a smile. "Come on, let's go see the old woman."

They walked a few yards along a narrow dirt road and spotted the hut just ahead. Just like the girl had said, the old woman sat in a chair in the hut, fanning herself with a piece of cardboard. She alternately whispered and talked to herself. When she saw the two strangers, she stopped muttering but continued fanning her dark, wrinkled face. She wore a traditional Indian dress that fit loosely over her thin, stooped frame.

"Hello. My name is Joe Coopersmith and this is Sarah Baker. We're from…"

"Where's your camera?"

"We're not tourists. And we didn't bring a camera."

"Well, the only reason people come to my hut is to take my picture. If you didn't bring a camera, why do you come here?"

"To ask you a few questions," Coopersmith answered. "The young woman at the curio shop said you knew a lot about the history of the village. We're trying to solve a family puzzle and we think maybe some of the pieces of that puzzle are right here in this village."

The old woman put down her fan. "Well, you came to the right place. I know everybody in the village and I know the history of the tribe better than anyone, even the smart ones who went to college and came back dumber than dirt. Why, if I had been able to go to school, I could've written a book about the Miccosukees. And I would've told the truth about how the white man drove us out into the middle of the everglades hoping the 'gators would eat us. Well, we taught everyone a lesson, didn't we? *We* wound up eating the 'gators and taming them too. Why, I can remember..."

"I'm sure you have a lot of interesting stories," Coopersmith interrupted. "And we'd like to listen to them after we talk about the matter we came to resolve. You see, we were hoping you might remember something that happened over sixty years ago."

"Let's see...I would've been in my twenties. There were lots more huts in those days. People still kept a lot of the customs. Not like today. The young kids watch TV, go to Miami every week; some even talk about leaving the tribe." She shook her head. "I don't know what's going to happen when the old ones like me, who know the ways of our forefathers, die off. And I'll tell you something else. The gambling places the Indians have built will be the end of us. You want to know why? They've made us dependent on money, just like the white man."

Sarah smiled and looked at Coopersmith.

"Like I started to say," Coopersmith said. "We'd like to know if you remember anything about a male baby or a child born here, but maybe taken out of the reservation to live somewhere else."

The old woman took a moment to think. "There was a young couple and a family with two girls that left during that time," she said, picking up the cardboard to fan herself again. "Don't know where the couple went, but the family came back a year later and then left again. Never did hear from them after that. The tribe is small and if a child had been taken away, like you said, to live outside the reservation, well, I think I would've remembered."

"This is very important," Sarah said. "Is it possible a young boy, maybe a teenager, could have run away and later chosen to live with a family outside the reservation?"

The old woman laughed. "You obviously don't know much about the Miccosukees. Indian boys don't run away. Besides, where can they run to, the Everglades? Or worse, Miami? No, whenever kids around here have problems, there's usually an elder, like myself or some strong tribal leader, who will talk to them and give them the right kind of advice."

"You're absolutely certain that no Indian boy has ever been raised outside the reservation," Coopersmith said.

The old woman nodded. "You seem disappointed."

"That's because I am. But you've been very patient with us and I thank you for taking the time to talk to us." He grinned and then added, "Maybe next time I'll bring my camera."

"Thank you," Sarah said, as she followed Coopersmith out of the hut.

They were almost at the car when Coopersmith paused and turned to look back toward the hut. "You know, it occurred to me that maybe we were asking the wrong questions."

"What do you mean?"

"Well, all along we were thinking that it was a baby or a young boy taken out of the tribe. What if a girl gave birth to a baby *after* she left the reservation."

"That would mean the baby could've been raised by almost anyone…even a black family."

"Let's go back and talk to her again," Coopersmith said, leading the way to the hut.

The woman acted surprised to see them back. "Did you forget something?" She put down her fan.

"Not exactly, but we do want to ask you one or two more questions," Coopersmith said. "That is if you don't mind."

The woman straightened up. "What kind of questions?"

"Do you remember any girl being pregnant and having to leave the reservation?" Sarah asked. "I'm sure girls back then, whether Indian or not, sometimes felt ostracized just because they got pregnant, usually by a boyfriend or someone who may have taken advantage of them."

"That has never happened," the old woman said. "The Miccosukees have always taken care of their own, and that includes babies born to innocent girls or to women who slept in another man's bed."

There was a brief silence. "Of course, there was that one girl who left the tribe," the old woman said. "She was six months pregnant and nobody knew who the father was. She eventually returned after she had a miscarriage." She paused for a moment. "Now that I think of it, there were some in the tribe who didn't believe her. There were even rumors she had given her baby away. But they were just rumors and eventually people forgot about it. She later got married, but she never had any children. She always wanted children, lots of them, but it was never meant to be." The old woman reached up to wipe a tear from her eye. "Such a long time ago. It made me sad just thinking about it."

"These rumors you talked about," Coopersmith said, "what were they exactly? There must have been a reason people didn't believe her?"

The woman considered the question. "There was no way of proving that…" She shook her head. "It was just a rumor. That's all."

"No way of proving what?" Sarah asked.

The woman suddenly got up with the help of a cane she kept next to her. "That after the baby's birth, she left him on the doorstep of a church," she said in a quiet, somber tone. "It's time for me to go inside and take a nap." She took a series of short steps as she slowly made her way out of the hut.

"Thank you," Sarah said.

"Thank you," echoed Coopersmith. They waited until the old woman shuffled inside the house and then slowly headed back to the car.

"So what do you think?" Sarah asked as they exited the village and turned onto the Trail.

"I'm not sure. Her last comment really got to me. She said it was just rumor, but it made me wonder."

"Yeah, me too. I guess we'll never know for sure, will we?"

"It doesn't look like it."

"Well, don't feel too bad. You followed your hunch and it just didn't pan out. I had to admit, though, for a moment I almost thought you were right. Not that it would have made any difference. I mean…well, you know what I'm trying to say."

Coopersmith looked at her and smiled. She was taking it better than him. He couldn't wait to drop her off so he could hurry back to his office to sort things out.

Thirty-Six

Sarah was the first to put it together and she couldn't wait to tell Coopersmith. When she called him at two o'clock in the morning and got no answer, she waited thirty seconds and tried again.

"This better not be a wrong number." Coopersmith sounded more sleepy than annoyed.

"I know it's late but I had to tell someone and…"

"Sarah?"

"I'm sorry I woke you, but I've been up for hours going over everything that happened yesterday afternoon. When I went to bed I started thinking of what the old woman said to us. Maybe I've been hanging around you too long, but I have a feeling she was holding back on us."

"You're calling me at two in the morning to tell me that?"

"Listen! The old woman used the word *him* when referring to the baby left in front of the church. How did she know it was a boy? And when she suddenly got up to leave, was it because she had said something that she wasn't supposed to? Maybe the rumors were true and the woman simply tried to protect the mother's reputation, even after all these years."

After a brief silence, Coopersmith said, "You know, I think you're on to something. Ever since I dropped you off, I've been playing the old what's-wrong-with-this-picture game, and still haven't come up with much."

"Then you agree we should go back there and ask more questions."

"Look, let me think about it and I'll call you in the morning."

"What is there to think about? You just said I was on to something."

"Okay, okay," he said, anxious to get back to sleep. "I'll pick you up at ten in the morning."

"I'll be ready at nine."

Sarah hadn't slept much, even after her phone call to Coopersmith. Unlike the day before, she seemed apprehensive.

"What if she doesn't want to see us again?" she said as they neared the Everglades.

"Relax. One way or another we'll get her to talk." As they approached Krome Avenue, Coopersmith put on his right blinker and slowed down to make the turn.

"Why are we turning here?" Sarah asked. "I thought we were going to the reservation."

"We are. There's a man we need to talk to for a few minutes. Before I left the house, I called Difalco to bounce a few theories off him and he told me about a fishing buddy, an old guy he used to know, who lives in a trailer just up ahead. He's a Miccosukee Indian who left the tribe to marry a white woman. They eventually got divorced but for some reason, he never went back to the reservation."

"What do you think the man will be able to tell us?"

"I'm not sure. Maybe nothing. He's not quite as old as Grandma, but he's old enough to remember a few things that might be useful when we talk to the old woman."

A few miles up the road, Coopersmith slowed down and began looking for a cluster of trailers set back behind tall trees and thick bushes.

"Look for a broken-down pickup filled with old tires and

junk. Difalco wasn't sure of the address, but he remembered the truck."

"There it is." Sarah pointed to the old, rusted truck just ahead.

Coopersmith slowed down and turned onto a dirt road where a few yards ahead, five or six trailers were barely visible behind a thicket of mangroves and tall palm trees. They pulled up slowly and parked in a graveled area off to the side and got out to look around.

"Good morning," Coopersmith said to a young, heavyset woman coming out of one of the trailers. She carried a large bag of trash and she turned to look at them.

"Morning." She dropped the bag into a tall metal trashcan and eyed them warily.

"We're looking for Johnny Tiger," Coopersmith said, walking up to her. "He's supposed to live in one of these trailers but I'm not sure which one."

"That's the Indian." She frowned. "Trailer number three. He's not very friendly, especially to strangers. Don't be surprised if he doesn't open the door."

"Thanks, I appreciate it," Coopersmith said. He and Sarah cut across a grassy area to the trailer with a big number 3 stenciled on its upper left side. Coopersmith knocked on the door, waited a few seconds, then knocked again. He walked around to the side and tapped on the window.

"My name is Joe Coopersmith and I'd like to talk to you," he shouted without knowing whether the old man could hear him. "I'm a friend of Ray Difalco. He said maybe you could help me with something." Coopersmith heard the front door opening and he hustled back to the front to see the old man standing half in and half out. He looked like the Indian on the old nickel, and he wore his salt and pepper hair in a long ponytail.

"If you're a friend of Ray Difalco, then you must be okay," he said in a semi-monotone. "What can I do for you?"

"May we come in?"

"Sure," he said, opening the door wider. Coopersmith and Sarah stepped in and took a seat on a small couch that had a Mexican serape draped over the back. The old man sat down across from them.

"Ray sends his regards. He promised to come see you the next time he makes it down here."

"It's been a long time since I've seen him," the old man said, a tinge of nostalgia in his voice. "We used to fish together, sometimes for hours, in every waterway for miles around. For a city boy, he sure took to the Everglades. Too bad he had to move so far away. The next time you see him, tell him I found a great spot on the other side of the reservation. Tell him he has to come and go fishing with me one last time before all the hairs on my head turn to silver."

Coopersmith smiled at the old man. "I'll be sure to tell him." He leaned forward. "The reason we came to see you is because we know you grew up on the reservation and you probably know everyone, especially some of the old folks like the woman called Grandma."

"You know Grandma?" he asked with a curious look.

"We went to see her yesterday to ask her some questions about a man we thought might be Sarah's father."

"A Miccosukee?" He turned to study Sarah's face as if to see if it were possible.

"That's what we're trying to find out," Coopersmith said. "The old lady told us about a pregnant young girl who had her baby outside the reservation. She said it was just a rumor, but we thought maybe she was trying to protect an old friend."

"You know about Grandma, don't you?"

Coopersmith and Sarah looked at each other. "What do you mean?" Sarah asked.

"She likes to make up stories, sometimes mixing the truth with Indian folklore or even some occasional gossip. She's interesting to listen to, but you can't take her too seriously. After a while it's hard to tell where the truth ends and her storytelling begins."

"But she had such a good memory," Sarah said, her voice rising slightly. "Why would she make up a rumor about something that happened over sixty years ago?"

The man crossed his arms. "She's just that way. After her husband died—and we're going back a long time ago—she started telling stories to the children in the tribe. It was her way of making up for the fact that she couldn't have children of her own. She really liked being every kid's second mother."

"And now she everyone's Grandma," Sarah said.

The man nodded. "That's right."

"Well, I think we've taken enough of your time," Coopersmith said, getting up to leave. He motioned to Johnny to remain seated. "We'll see ourselves out."

"Thank you," Sarah said as she followed Coopersmith.

The two were almost at the door, when the old man suddenly stood up and called out Sarah's name. "You have it," he said.

Sarah turned to him with a puzzled frown.

"You have the look," he said as though he were making a proclamation.

"I know what you're thinking, Sarah," Coopersmith said when they were back in the car traveling south on Krome. "But it's too far-fetched."

"You're right," she said, nodding. "Then again when you think of it, stranger things have happened since you first started delving into people's lives." For the rest of the short drive to the village, Sarah remained quiet, her mind still on the old man's description of Grandma and especially his parting words.

When they pulled into the parking lot of the curio shop, they sat in the car and waited a moment. "This time I'm a little afraid and I'm not sure why, exactly," Sarah said, turning to Coopersmith.

"I think I know the reason. Part of you really doesn't want to know the truth. Not that I blame you. If I were in your shoes,

I'm not sure I wouldn't be having the same feelings."

Sarah smiled at him. "Thanks for being so understanding. It makes me feel a little better." She took a deep breath. "Let's do it." She reached for the door.

Grandma sat in the same spot as before, and she turned to them when she heard their steps getting closer. When she saw Sarah enter the hut, she reached for her cane and pushed herself to her feet. She had been expecting them, it seemed, and her eyes quickly filled with tears that trickled down her wrinkled brown face.

"I knew you'd be back," she said, her lips quivering uncontrollably. "I wanted to tell you, but I was afraid of what you would think of me."

Sarah hesitated, then started to cry as she reached out to put her arms around the old woman. "It's okay…Grandmother. It's okay. We've found each other and that's all that matters. Everything's going to be just fine."

"I'm still on a kind of high," Sarah said as they drove back to Miami. "To find my natural grandmother and discover I'm part Miccosukee all in a couple of days. It's bizarre and it's wonderful. I didn't get to thank you back there, so I just want to say that I really appreciate what you did for me. If you hadn't followed your hunch about the face in the poster, well…"

"I'm just glad everything turned out okay."

Sarah became quiet. "I know you probably won't agree with me, but I think my sister and brothers should know the truth. It just wouldn't be fair to keep this kind of thing from them."

"Fair?" Coopersmith said with a raised eyebrow. "The way I see it, they don't deserve to know the truth. Not now, not ever, except for Daniel. Do me a favor. Think about it and don't do anything for a while."

Sarah smiled at him. "I'll think about it and I promise I won't do anything before telling you. After all you've done, I owe you that much, at least."

Coopersmith smiled back and pressed the accelerator to get

around a large truck towing a sleek racing boat with the name *Indian Princess* painted on its side. When they saw it, they turned to each other and laughed.

Coopersmith didn't hear from Sarah until late the next day. She had just talked with Mark and sounded a little down.

"Mark thought it was great news," she said. "I told him all about it. He thinks now we can patch things up and put it all behind us."

"Is that what you want to do?"

"I know what you're thinking. To tell you the truth, I can't see us getting back together. When he said that being part Indian was not as bad, I suddenly realized I never really knew him." She sighed. "Funny how you think you know someone until something like this happens and you find out who they really are."

"Well, whatever happens, I wish you luck. I'll be around if you need me and even if you don't, I hope you'll give me a call now and then…just to say hello."

"You can count it." She hesitated for a second. "I never thought I'd say this, especially now that I've found my grandmother. But… if I had it to do over again, I'm not sure I would. Maybe you were right. Some things *are* better left alone."

New York City

The caller's voice was muffled and had a Southern twang that didn't sound real.

"What? What did you say?" Brewster asked, his ear pressed tightly against the receiver. "I can't understand you."

The caller's voice became clearer. "You didn't think it was over, did you?" He let out a laugh. "Listen carefully. I got the briefcase and the pictures and I know all about your black father. Why don't you make it easy on yourself and do exactly as I say?"

"This can't be happening," Brewster's voice broke into a

squeak. "It's some joke, isn't it? Tell me this is somebody's idea of a fucking joke."

After a short silence the caller dropped his phony accent. "The joke's on you, asshole. If you don't come up with fifty grand by this time next week, the whole town's going to know all about your dark little secret. You got a lot to lose, more than you did in Atlanta, so don't disappoint me."

"Who is this?"

Dead silence.

"Damn it, who is this?" Brewster yelled. "I have to know. Who is this? Who is this?"

AUTHOR ERNESTO PATINO

Ernesto Patino grew up in El Paso, Texas, and worked for 23 years as an FBI agent. He lives in Tucson, Arizona, where he divides his time between writing and working as a private investigator. His previous novel, *In the Shadow of a Stranger,* was published in England and he is currently at work on a new novel set in South Florida where he lived for 22 years prior to moving to Arizona.